D0427699

What is wrong with Star?

Cindy was just stepping outside. Her face looked softer and less stressed than it had since she'd come home. She leaned on the door of the stall, watching as Christina offered Star a warm bucket of mash.

"I've spent so much time exercise riding and racing," Cindy said, "I'd forgotten what it's like to just spend time with a horse." She shook her head when Star turned up his nose at the bucket of food. "Don't let him fool you, Chris," Cindy said. "He hasn't given up yet."

"Thanks," Christina said, amazed at the change in Cindy. She put down the bucket and ran her hand along Star's neck. His skin was loose, a clear sign of dehydration. Christina pulled his ear affectionately, but Star didn't react.

The faint spark of hope Cindy's words had kindled was instantly smothered. Star appeared to be getting worse.

Collect all the books in the Thoroughbred series

THOROUGHBRED Super Editions

ASHLEIGH'S Thoroughbred Collection

* coming soon

THOROUGHBRED

FALLEN STAR

CREATED BY
JOANNA CAMPBELL

WRITTEN BY
MARY NEWHALL ANDERSON

HarperEntertainment
An Imprint of HarperCollinsPublishers

HarperEntertainment

An Imprint of HarperCollins*Publishers*

10 East 53rd Street, New York, NY 10022

This is a work of fiction. The characters, incidents, and dialogues are products of the author's imagination and are not to be construed as real. Any resemblance to actual events or persons, living or dead, is entirely coincidental.

Produced by 17th Street Productions, an Alloy Online, Inc. company

HarperCollins books are available at special quantity discounts for bulk purchases for sales promotions, premiums, or fund-raising. For information, please call or write: Special Markets Department, HarperCollins Publishers Inc., 10 East 53rd Street, New York, NY 10022. Telephone: (212) 207-7528. Fax: (212) 207-7222.

ISBN 0–06–105874–2

HarperCollins®, ﹏®, and HarperEntertainment™ are trademarks of HarperCollins Publishers Inc.

Cover art © 2000 by 17th Street Productions, an Alloy Online, Inc. company

First printing: October 2000

Printed in the United States of America

Visit HarperEntertainment on the World Wide Web at www.harpercollins.com

❖ 10 9 8 7 6 5 4 3 2 1

*To the wonderful girls
of the Thoroughbred series
fan clubs on egroups*

"WE'RE HERE, STAR," CHRISTINA REESE CALLED OUT.

The rising sun was barely a sliver of light on the horizon as she stepped from the taxi near the back gate to New York's Belmont racetrack. She waited impatiently while her parents, Ashleigh Griffen and Mike Reese, paid the driver.

"We're going to get a cup of coffee," her mother said, joining her. "Do you want to come with us?"

Christina shook her head. "I'm going straight to Star's stall," she replied. The Reeses had just flown up to New York from Kentucky for the weekend, but Wonder's Star, their two-year-old Thoroughbred colt, had been at Belmont for nearly a week. Christina hated being away from Star, but she knew it was important for the colt to have a chance to adjust to the new setting

1

before she raced him on Sunday. Now that she was here in New York, too, she couldn't wait to see Star.

"We'll be over to his stall in a while," Mike said, draping his arm over Ashleigh's shoulders.

Her parents headed for the track kitchen, and Christina strode toward the barns, eager to get to her colt. Even though it was barely five o'clock on Saturday morning, the backside hummed with activity. Christina made her way around grooms pushing wheelbarrows of soiled bedding and past sleek Thoroughbreds being tacked up for their morning works. From some of the stalls came the soft rustling and crunching sounds of horses eating their breakfast hay, while the clattering of dancing hooves, loud snorts, and excited whinnies carried through the cool air of the late September dawn.

When she neared the stall assigned to Whitebrook, her parents' farm, Christina could see Star's copper-colored nose pointing in her direction. The chestnut colt gave a throaty nicker when he spotted her. She sped up, covering the last several yards at a brisk pace. She slipped inside the stall and wrapped her arms around Star's neck. The colt nuzzled her, clearly happy to see her.

"Oh, Star," she murmured, running her hand along his shoulder. "I really missed you, boy. I wish I could have been here to help you get settled, but I know Dani's been taking good care of you."

2

Star felt warm, his smooth coat sleek and soft. Christina pressed her face into his neck, inhaling his scent deeply. Star lipped at her hair, chuffing warm, heavy breaths into her ear, making Christina laugh.

"Of course I brought you something, spoiled boy!" She dug into her jeans pocket, producing a handful of carrot chunks. Star happily crunched on the treats while Christina stroked his sleek, muscular neck.

Christina was Star's jockey, while Brad Townsend and Christina's parents shared the colt's ownership. Still, Christina would always think of Star as her own. If only that were so.

Christina's dream was to earn enough money to buy the half interest in Star held by Brad Townsend. Townsend Acres was the farm where Star's dam, Ashleigh's Wonder, had been bred. Every one of Wonder's offspring, including Star, was half owned by the Townsends. Christina wanted to break that tradition. But first she needed to convince Brad and Lavinia Townsend to sell their interest in Star, which was close to impossible. Then she had to have the money. Even by saving every penny of the purses she had been winning as a jockey, it could take her a lifetime to earn enough. But, she comforted herself, massaging Star's poll, at least she was able to race the colt, who was rapidly gaining a reputation for his ability on the track.

Star finished his carrots and began nuzzling Christina all over, searching for more. "That's it, greedy." She laughed fondly, rubbing the white star on the colt's gleaming forehead, and glanced around his stall. Star's groom, Dani Martens, had already given him fresh water, and his full hay net hung in the corner.

"Hi there."

Christina looked up to see Cindy McLean at the stall door. The adopted daughter of Whitebrook's head trainer, Cindy was a well-known jockey in New York. Cindy had grown up at Whitebrook, but Christina had been only four when she left, so she barely knew the small blond woman, although she had heard a lot about her. Ashleigh had arranged for Cindy to work Star during the week, while Christina was at school.

"He's all set to race tomorrow," Cindy said approvingly. "It was a real kick to work him for you this week. It's been almost twelve years since I rode a horse for Whitebrook. I wouldn't mind racing him tomorrow myself."

"Star's pretty amazing," Christina agreed. "I can't wait to show him off tomorrow. We're going to win, aren't we, boy?"

Cindy raised her eyebrows. "He's a strong runner," she said. "But don't get too arrogant. You never know what could happen during a race."

Christina shifted Star's light sheet, settling it smoothly on his back. "I'm not worried," she said confidently. "Everyone is saying he's a sure thing for the Kentucky Derby. Tomorrow's race is just one more chance for Star to prove himself."

"I hope you're right," Cindy said. "And if you ever need a replacement jockey for him, just let me know."

"Thanks for offering," Christina said, flashing Cindy a quick smile. "But I hope I'll be able to ride him in all of his races." She glanced at her watch. "You get back to your breakfast, Star," she said, giving the colt a parting rub. "I'm going to check on Gratis." She stepped out of the stall and latched the door.

"Don't you have any horses to work this morning?" she asked Cindy. "At home it seems like I'm on the track breezing nonstop until they close it for the races." Since most jockeys took advantage of exercise riding to keep in shape and get to know the horses they were going to race, it surprised Christina that Cindy, a regular jockey at Belmont, didn't have a bunch of horses to ride that morning.

Cindy tucked her short blond hair behind her ears and shrugged. "Not this morning," she said, glancing around the stabling area. "I'm taking it easy for this afternoon. I have three races scheduled. That should wear me out."

"It'll be great to see you ride," Christina said.

"Just another day on the job," Cindy said casually. But Christina heard an edge of excitement in

Cindy's voice, and she understood it. Although she'd been racing for a year, she always felt a thrill before a race. Lucky for her she had a warm-up before Star's race the next day—she would be racing Gratis for Vince Jones in only a few hours.

They crossed the wide aisle to where Vince Jones's horses were stabled. Vince, one of the top trainers in the United States, had brought Star up from Kentucky for the Reeses, along with several other horses he was working for his clients.

"Gratis must be getting a bath," Christina said when she peered into the bay colt's empty stall. "I haven't talked to Vince yet, since we got here so late last night. I hope Gratis's exercise rider didn't have too much trouble with him this week." Christina started for the end of the shed row, Cindy beside her.

"I didn't hear any of the other jockeys complaining about him," Cindy said. "He must not have been too rambunctious."

"That's good," Christina said. "I don't want to fight him this afternoon. Vince still isn't so sure he should have a bug racing for him. I'm just lucky Gratis decided he would put up with me."

They found the big bay colt tied at the wash rack. Gratis kept twisting his head as he tried to keep a wild-looking eye on the groom who was bathing him.

The girl shot Christina a pained look. "I think you

and Mrs. Graber are the only people in the world this horse likes," she said, rubbing her soapy wash mitt against the handsome colt's glistening wet shoulder. She took a quick step back as Gratis stamped his front foot, missing her booted toe by inches. "See what I mean?" She glared at the irascible colt, who pinned his ears in response.

"Knock it off!" Cindy snapped at Gratis, taking a bold step toward the horse. Gratis's ears flicked forward and back and he stared at Cindy, who shook her head in disgust.

Christina froze, shocked at Cindy's tone. Then she stepped forward, holding out her hand. "You're just a big fake, aren't you?" she said sweetly. Gratis swiveled his head toward her, and she rubbed his jaw with her fingertips. He took a quick nip at her arm, his lips popping together just short of her skin.

"You know better than that," she scolded gently, giving the corner of his mouth a flick with her fingers. Gratis snapped his head up. Christina tried not to chuckle at the colt's shocked expression. Gratis was smart and fast on the track but had few manners to speak of. His owner, Fredericka Graber, hated to see her horses disciplined in any way. Christina knew a horse that didn't respect its handlers could be dangerous, but Gratis responded well to gentleness.

She turned to the groom. "He looks great," she said

to the girl. "I'll see you in the walking ring, big guy." She gave the colt's nose a quick rub before turning away.

"I know he's fast, but he's a little too spoiled for my taste," Cindy commented, frowning. "I hope you don't let him push you around."

"Of course not!" Christina said quickly. "I can handle him just fine." She didn't know why Cindy was making such a big deal out of it. Gratis hadn't done anything wrong.

"I see the colt from the United Arab Emirates, Rush Street, is racing against him today," Cindy commented. "Gratis had better be on top of his game."

"Rush Street? I haven't heard anything about him," Christina said.

"I'm not surprised," Cindy said, dropping onto a folding chair in front of Star's stall. "Even though he was Kentucky bred, he's been in training in Dubai. They just brought him back to race him."

Christina leaned against Star's door. The handsome colt rested his jaw on her shoulder, and Christina wrapped her arm around his neck, rubbing his ear affectionately. "Gratis is almost as fast as Star," she said. "That other colt won't be able to touch him."

Cindy wrinkled her nose. "Rush Street's trainer, Connie Richmond, is right up there with Vince Jones for being a top-rated conditioner."

8

"How come no one talks about her?" Christina frowned. "Everyone knows Vince. He's always being interviewed about his wins in the Triple Crown races and which horses he thinks are the top ones. He has a lot of confidence in Gratis. No one can touch him."

Cindy rolled her eyes. "Don't be too cocky, Chris. Vince Jones isn't the only trainer in the world to produce a winning horse," she said. "Maybe you should talk to him about Rush Street before you decide that Gratis has already won today's race."

Christina stiffened at Cindy's harsh words, but she knew the other jockey was right. She'd been so focused on visiting with the horses, she hadn't thought about much else. "What else do you know about Rush Street?" she asked.

"His times have been consistently impressive," Cindy said. "It isn't going to be an easy race."

"Maybe you're right," Christina said dubiously. "I guess I'd better go talk to Vince."

"I'm going to find your mom and dad," Cindy said. "I haven't had a chance to talk to them yet."

Christina found Vince Jones at the track, a stopwatch in one hand and a clipboard in the other. His gaze was fixed on a gray colt jogging along the outside edge of the racetrack. Christina rested her forearms on the rail, mimicking the gruff old trainer's pose.

"Gratis is good and ready for this afternoon," Vince

said without even looking up. "He was no angel this week, but he's acted much worse. I'm sure he'll be fine for you."

"What about the number six horse?" Christina asked.

"The big bay from Dubai." Vince narrowed his eyes. "He could give Gratis some trouble. You'll know him when you see him—seventeen-point-three hands and all legs, looks more like a giraffe than a horse. But when he gets moving it's like watching a steam engine roll down the track. I saw one of his works the other day. Pretty darned amazing."

"Well, Gratis is pretty amazing, too," Christina said, her confidence wavering slightly.

Vince shot her a stern look. "You need to be on your toes this afternoon, Chris."

"Okay," Christina said, watching the gray colt Vince was timing turn along the inside rail.

"I'll see you at the paddock," Vince said, dismissing her. He waved his watch at the exercise rider, who shifted forward and cued his mount to break into a gallop. Christina watched the horse run a five-furlong breeze, then she returned to the barn. Dani was sitting near Star's stall, rerolling a pile of leg wraps. She had headphones on and was bobbing her head in time to some music. She nodded a greeting to Christina.

"Hey, spoiled boy," Christina called. Star blew noisily and turned around, sticking his head into the aisle. "I love you, you big silly," she murmured. "I'll bring you a big, juicy apple after I'm done with Gratis, okay?"

She noticed a groom leading a black horse in their direction, and she tapped Dani's shoulder. The groom pulled her headphones down, letting them hang from her neck.

"Who is that?" Christina asked, nodding toward the approaching colt.

"Fire 'n' Ice," Dani said. "He came in Thursday. He's in the stall next to Star's, but he's really quiet. It's been kind of nice, having a mellow horse next door."

The colt walked slowly up the aisle, his head low. "He's sure laid-back," Christina commented to the colt's handler. "Is he all right?"

The groom opened the stall door and led the colt inside. "He's been a little sluggish since his last race in Florida," he said. "But the vet thinks he's just having a hard time adjusting after the trip. He's usually calm anyway, so we're not too worried."

"Does he have a lot of wins?" Christina asked, gazing at the white stripe running down the colt's nose. He looked at her indifferently.

"He's had two third-place finishes out of five starts," the groom said. "He's supposed to race again Tuesday." He latched the stall door and slung the lead line over his shoulder. "Bye now," he said, and walked away.

Ashleigh, Mike, and Cindy came down the aisle, engrossed in conversation. They stopped at Star's stall.

"Are you ready to weigh in?" Cindy asked Christina. "I'll go with you to the jockeys' lounge."

"We'll see you both at the track," Ashleigh said, giving Christina a quick hug. "Good luck."

As she and Cindy headed for the jockeys' lounge, Christina noticed a slight frown puckering Cindy's brow, and when Cindy shifted her backpack on her left shoulder, a look of pain flickered across her face.

"Are you all right?" Christina asked, concerned.

Cindy's face cleared immediately. She took a deep breath and offered Christina a bright smile. "I'm fine," she said. "I was just thinking about all the races I've ridden here over the years." She moved her shoulder and wrinkled her nose. "And all my bumps and bruises," she added with a laugh.

"Which race was the best?" Christina asked curiously.

"Any of them I won," Cindy casually. "Although the Belmont Stakes had to be the greatest, even if I never came close to winning."

Christina struggled to remember what year Cindy had ridden in the Belmont Stakes. She wasn't even sure she had watched the race. Until recently, Christina's heart had been set on three-day eventing. But once she started working with Star and had experienced the thrill of racing, she realized it was her true passion. Eventually she had sold her eventing horse, Sterling Dream, and now she was completely focused on building her career as a jockey.

"Cindy McLean! Hold on a second!" A tall blond man with a bushy mustache was striding across the grounds, a press pass clipped to his jacket. "I'm glad I caught you," he said to Cindy, then darted a look at Christina. "Cindy McLean's a hard person to get a quote from, you know." He held up a small tape recorder and looked at Cindy hopefully.

"Hi, Randy," Cindy said flatly. "I guess I never have anything to say that's worth printing." She pressed her lips together, clearly unwilling to say more.

"Oh." Randy fixed his pale blue eyes on Christina and grinned broadly. "Christina Reese," he said, holding out the recorder. "How do you feel about racing Gratis today?"

"I'm looking forward to it," Christina answered confidently. "There are some strong runners, and it should be an exciting race."

"I hear Vince has Gratis running in the Futurity, but your mother isn't racing Star until the Champagne Stakes. What's the deal with that?" Randy asked.

"Two different trainers, two different schedules," Christina said neutrally.

"You sound like you're quoting this morning's paper," Randy complained. "I heard the same statements from Vince Jones and Ashleigh Griffen earlier. I want to hear *your* thoughts. Why are you the only rider Vince will name on Gratis? He's never used a bug before. Why now?"

"Gratis works well for me," Christina said, proud of herself for keeping her cool.

"Do you think your apprentice allowance is helping Gratis win?"

Until she won forty-five races and had been racing for a year, Christina would be an apprentice jockey, or "bug." In some races bugs were given a weight allowance, meaning they carried less weight than the riders who had lost their bug. Since she had already won several races, Christina's allowance was at five pounds, where it would stay until her year was up.

"Gratis could win even without the allowance," she said quickly. "He—"

"We need to get inside," Cindy said, interrupting her. She moved between Christina and the reporter. "Come on, Christina, you're going to be late."

"What about Star?" the reporter demanded, leaning around Cindy. "It seems to me he's run into trouble in almost every one of his races. Yet there's talk you

14

folks have him pinned for the Derby. Do you *really* think he has a shot at it?"

Christina caught her breath as Cindy steered her toward the door. Randy sped up, keeping step with them.

"Star is ready for tomorrow," Christina said, giving the reporter a hard look. "We'll do fine."

Cindy grabbed the door handle to the jockeys' lounge. "Off-limits, Randy," she said, putting her hand on Christina's shoulder. "Come on, Chris, let's go inside."

"Star doesn't seem to be quite the horse Gratis is," the reporter called out before Christina could get through the door. "He's more of a slacker than the brilliant racehorse his dam was. Do you really think he has what it takes to be as great as Wonder? Do you really put Wonder's Star in the same category as Gratis or Rush Street?"

Christina bristled. An image of Star thundering along the rail, running with all his heart, flashed through her mind. She shrugged Cindy's hand off her shoulder and whipped around to face the reporter.

"Star is the most magnificent horse I've ever ridden," she said fiercely. "He's smart, he's strong, and he's determined. I'm riding him because he does his best for me. I guarantee you we'll be in the starting gate with the best of the best next May at Churchill Downs. You can count on it."

15

She heard Cindy's sharp intake of breath and snapped her mouth shut.

"That's great! Thanks a lot! Later, ladies," Randy quipped.

Christina winced as the reporter hurried off. She pressed her hand to her mouth and closed her eyes.

"Too late for that now," Cindy said dryly. "Just hope he doesn't get a big headline to match the big words."

Christina groaned. "I can't believe I walked right into that."

Cindy shrugged. "You'll learn to keep your mouth shut. Randy did the same thing to me the year Arctic Sun and I came in second at the Wood Memorial and Cedar Slewth and I missed winning the Peter Pan Stakes by a length. When I blew it on Catapullet in the Travers Stakes, I swore I'd never talk to another reporter again. I felt like I was jinxed because I bragged so much about my horses."

Christina felt her jaw go slack as Cindy rattled off famous horses and races as though they were nothing. "You've ridden in a lot of great races, haven't you?"

Cindy nodded, pushing the door open. "And that was just in the States," she said with a grin, stepping inside. It didn't sound to Christina as though Cindy minded bragging. She dropped the name of a big race or a great horse every chance she got. There was something about Cindy that Christina wasn't sure she liked.

Christina glanced around the spacious lounge as the door fell shut behind them. Several jockeys were seated on soft chairs around a big-screen television, and Christina recognized a pair of well-known jockeys playing a game of pool. A few riders greeted Cindy by name and nodded politely to Christina as they made their way to the women's dressing room.

By the time she had weighed in, handed her saddle off to Dani, and dressed in the green-and-purple silks of Tall Oaks, the first race of the day was being run. The sound of the announcer's voice rang through the jockeys' lounge, and Christina sat down in front of the television to watch. Cindy was riding in the second race, so she had already headed for the track.

When the call to the post sounded, Christina watched closely as Cindy and her gray filly came onto the track. She knew she could learn a lot from watching an experienced jockey such as Cindy, whether she liked her or not.

But from the moment the horses broke from the gate, Christina could tell Cindy was in trouble. She hunched stiffly over the filly's shoulders, and Christina watched her pass up several chances to maneuver ahead of the pack.

Christina gripped her hands together, willing Cindy to make a move. Finally, as they neared the end of the race, a clear gap opened. Cindy reached back to tap her mount's hip with her whip. Christina saw Cindy flinch and freeze before she could finish swinging her arm. It was obvious that only Cindy's skillful riding kept her from pitching off the filly's back. She finished the race in fifth place.

The rest of the riders began to return to the lounge, but Christina had to leave for her own race before she saw Cindy. She walked through the tunnel that led to the track with the rest of the jockeys, their footsteps echoing hollowly in the silence. They emerged into a large yard near the viewing ring.

Fredericka Graber waited at the mounting spot for Gratis's gate position, number seven. The colt's owner wore a linen suit matching the colors of her farm, Tall Oaks.

"Good luck, Christina," the owner said. She gave Christina's arm a nervous squeeze, her attention on the saddling area, where Gratis was giving Vince and the handler some trouble.

Christina laughed at the colt's antics. "Well, he looks ready to go."

Fredericka smiled kindly. "I'm sure you and Gratis will be magnificent," she said.

"Thanks," Christina said, buckling her chin strap. "I'll do my best."

Finally Vince strode up to them and nodded at

Fredericka. "Your colt looks good," he said, all business. Then he turned to Christina. "You know what to do, right? Keep him inside, behind the leaders. Don't press him. Let him find his rhythm. When you see something open up, don't wait for someone else to take it. Go for it."

"Yes, sir," Christina said. She watched Rush Street as the colt was led by, the number six emblazoned on his saddle blanket. The colt was enormous, his gait so extended that he seemed to float around the viewing ring. She clenched her jaw. If he ran the way he walked, she and Gratis had their work cut out for them.

"Watch the traffic out there," Vince said, giving her a leg up onto Gratis's back. Her parents were standing outside the walking ring, and Christina waved to them, warmed by the proud smiles she saw on their faces. Then she and Gratis headed toward the track for the post parade.

As they lined up behind the starting gate Christina settled her helmet forward and adjusted her goggles.

Gratis snorted, pawed, and rocked impatiently as the gate closed behind him. Christina knew he was eager to get onto the track. Finally the last horse was loaded, and she prepared herself for the explosive start. There was a split second of stillness. Christina felt Gratis tense beneath her, every muscle like a coiled spring.

Then the gate banged open, and they surged onto the track. Gratis broke well, strong and straight as an arrow. Christina dropped the colt to the rail, trying to hold him back behind the leaders. The eager two-year-old strained against the reins, fighting to run at the front of the pack. Christina braced herself against him, willing the spirited horse to ease up. They had plenty of time to overpower the rest of the field. Gratis fought her with every stride, and Christina gave up, letting him fly past the other horses to the front of the pack.

But the bay colt beside them seemed to have the same drive that Gratis did. Christina shot a quick glance to her left. Rush Street was neck and neck with Gratis. He seemed to be running easily. His jockey, wearing black-and-silver silks, curled his lip at Christina as he guided Rush Street along the track, matching Gratis stride for stride. A glance behind them showed the rest of the field several lengths back, and Christina could hear the announcer's voice over the horses' pounding hooves.

"It's Gratis and Rush Street vying for the lead!" his voice rang overhead. "Sir Real is in third, with the rest of the field trailing well behind!"

By the time they reached the fourth pole, Christina knew the race was between Gratis and Rush Street. She saw the other jockey lift his whip and flick it past the colt's line of vision. In response, Rush Street stretched out. His burst of speed made it seem as though he hadn't even been trying before.

"No!" Christina exclaimed, horrified. She focused on the view between Gratis's ears and pressed her fists into his mane, urging him on. Gratis eagerly picked up his pace, pounding down the stretch beside Rush

Street. Christina felt the tremendous power in the bay colt's muscles, and she did everything she could to help him along.

"Come on, boy!" she cried, feeling Gratis pouring energy into each forceful stride. She settled into a tight crouch, letting the colt run the race. They kept up with Rush Street, matching his driving strides.

Christina counted lengths and watched the furlong markers fly past. As they bore down on the finish line she rose in her stirrups and balanced precariously over Gratis's pumping shoulders, all her weight balanced between her toes and her knees.

"Come on, Gratis!" she called urgently. "This is it!" The colt leaped forward mightily, winning the race by only half a stride.

Christina couldn't tell if the roaring in her ears was the blood rushing through her veins or the shouting of the crowd. She sat back, trying to slow Gratis down, but the energetic colt struggled to keep running, and they cantered sideways for several steps until the outrider caught them and helped her bring Gratis under control.

"That was pretty exciting," the outrider commented as he escorted them back to the grandstand, where Vince and Fredericka were waiting by the winner's circle.

"Tell me about it," Christina gasped, exhausted

from the effort of keeping the headstrong colt in line during the race.

"Wonderful!" Fredericka exclaimed, beaming happily at Christina when she stepped into the circle. "What a thrilling race! I think I held my breath the entire time!"

Vince let a small smile flicker across his dour face. "Good job," he said, giving her a nod of approval. To Christina, those two words were lavish praise.

As she moved Gratis into place for the photographer, Christina saw her parents and Cindy standing outside the winner's circle. Mike and Ashleigh smiled and waved, but Cindy looked glum, her eyes downcast. Christina felt sorry for her.

"Miss Reese?" the photographer called. She turned back to smile for the camera, then hopped from Gratis's back and started toward the backside. Gratis was the only horse she was racing today, and she was eager to change into her regular clothes and spend more time with Star.

"Excuse me, Miss Reese?"

Christina stopped and turned to face a tall, dark-haired man. "Yes?" she responded, eyeing him curiously.

"My name is Ben al-Rihani," he said. "I wanted to congratulate you on a magnificent ride. I was quite impressed to see you hand-ride to win over my prize colt."

Christina grinned at him, swinging her helmet by its strap. "I'd apologize for winning, Mr. al-Rihani, but it wouldn't be very sincere. Gratis earned that win."

Ben al-Rihani smiled warmly. "Please, call me Ben," he said. "And yes, you and that colt did earn your win. But my trainer and I will be watching for you and your clever strategies."

Christina glanced down at her dirt-spattered nylon breeches and tugged at the goggles hanging around her neck. "I really need to go change," she said. "It was nice meeting you. And beating your colt," she added with a grin.

Ben laughed. "Just wait until the next race," he said. "I believe you'll be riding Gratis in the Futurity in a couple of weeks. My trainer has Rush Street in that race as well. Then we'll see whose colt is the better one, right?"

Christina nodded. "We'll see," she said. "It was nice talking to you," she added, then headed for the dressing room.

After she changed, she found her parents and Cindy waiting for her near the grandstand.

"Congratulations!" Ashleigh said, hugging Christina tightly. "You were amazing, Chris. Just amazing!"

Her father tugged her ponytail. "You should be very proud of yourself, sweetheart."

Cindy forced a thin smile. "You did a great job, Chris," she said. "That will definitely be a video you won't mind watching during the race reviews."

Christina rolled her eyes. The apprentice jockeys had daily meetings with the track officials, where they watched tapes of their races and had their performances evaluated. "There have been times I could have just died from embarrassment watching myself," she admitted.

"Me too," Ashleigh said, laughing.

Cindy hesitated, then nodded. "I've had a few of those races too."

"Is your shoulder okay?" Christina asked. "I was worried. It looked like it was really bothering you."

Cindy's expression darkened. "It's a little sore," she said. "Nothing serious, but the track doctor ordered me not to ride for a few weeks. No big deal." Cindy shrugged.

Christina frowned. Not ride for a few weeks? It sounded like a big deal to her.

"So what are you up to now?" Cindy asked, clearly wanting to change the subject.

"I'm going to call Melanie and tell her about the race," Christina said. She was eager to share her news with her best friend and cousin, Melanie Graham, who was also an apprentice jockey. "Then I'm going to groom Star."

25

"What about Parker?" Mike asked. "Aren't you going to call him, too?"

A smile tugged at Christina's mouth at the mention of her boyfriend, Parker Townsend. "He's at a schooling show with some of his students," she said. "I have to wait until tomorrow to talk to him."

"Don't forget we're having dinner with Fredericka tonight," Ashleigh reminded her.

"I won't," Christina said. She started away, then turned back to ask her mother what time they were supposed to meet Gratis's owner. But Christina decided not to bother them when she saw her mother and Cindy talking in low voices and her father's face creased with worry. Something was definitely up.

"I don't know what's going on, Mel," Christina said, squeezing the telephone receiver between her ear and her shoulder. She perched on the edge of Vince Jones's small desk, swinging her foot absently as she gazed out the open door of the stall Vince was using for an office.

"Didn't your mom say Cindy hurt her shoulder when she was riding for Whitebrook?" Melanie asked.

"But that was a long time ago. I was only three when she got hurt," Christina said, picking at a hangnail on her thumb. She angled her head so that she could see Star's stall. Only the colt's sleek hip showed over the door. "She's been racing for years since then."

"I don't know what to tell you, Chris," Melanie said. "Hey, I have to go. Kevin is waiting for me to get off the phone so we can drive up to Turfway."

"Is he going to let you drive?" Christina asked. She and Melanie were taking driver education, and both grabbed every chance they could to get behind the wheel. Kevin McLean, who was the son of White-brook's head trainer, Ian, and who was also Melanie's ex-boyfriend, let them drive his truck every once in a while, but it made him extremely nervous.

"I doubt it," Melanie said. "He just wants to visit Image with me."

Melanie had been working with another of Freder-icka Graber's young horses, Perfect Image, a beautiful black filly with an even bigger attitude problem than Gratis. Melanie had her work cut out for her if she hoped to make the swift but flighty filly into a success-ful racehorse.

"I'll see you tomorrow when I get back," Christina said, returning the phone to the cradle. She crossed the aisle to Star's stall. The colt pushed his nose in her direction, arching his neck as she rubbed her hands along his crest. Christina could certainly understand Melanie's infatuation with Image. She felt the same way about Star. No horse could ever replace him.

"Are you ready for tomorrow, boy?" she asked. "After the way I bragged to that reporter this morning, we'd better do well." She sighed and raked her fingers through Star's gleaming mane. "You will anyway, right? You'll do it for me, won't you, Star? Not for some dumb newspaper."

Star bobbed his head, and Christina laughed. "You'll do it just because you love to run, right?" She turned away from Star's stall to see Gratis's groom walking him back to his stall after his postrace bath. The colt bowed his neck, prancing as if he was ready to run again. Fredericka Graber approached the stall from the other end of the aisle, brandishing a shiny red apple.

"How is my Gratis doing after his run this afternoon?" Fredericka asked the colt in a sweet, singsong voice.

Gratis whinnied loudly when he saw Fredericka, nearly jerking the lead line from the groom's hand. The handler quickly maneuvered the colt into his stall and closed the door.

"The poor horse is hungry," Fredericka said. "He just wants a bite to eat, don't you, sweetie?"

Christina joined Fredericka at Gratis's stall. "The trouble is," Christina said, "he doesn't care if it's a groom's arm or an apple that he bites into."

The bay colt pawed his bedding and gave an impatient snort. Fredericka gazed fondly at her cranky, spoiled horse. "But he's such a magnificent runner, it makes up for his bad manners," she said. "You did such a marvelous job with him this afternoon."

"It was a good race," Christina agreed.

"You're going to be my Derby winner, aren't you," Fredericka crooned to Gratis. She held out the apple she'd been carrying. The colt lifted the apple from her hand and chewed it noisily, then pressed his muzzle against her palm and snuffled it. Fredericka treated the horse the way a mother would her precocious child. And Gratis seemed to respond to Fredericka the same way. Christina had never seen him pin his ears or bare his teeth at her.

"And with you on him in the Derby, Christina," Fredericka continued, "he'll be unstoppable."

Christina gnawed at her lower lip. How could she tell Fredericka she expected to ride Star in the Derby? *Next May is still a long way off*, she reminded herself. There was plenty of time to figure out who was riding what horse in the Derby.

"I want you to have this," Fredericka said, pulling an envelope from her handbag and handing it to Christina. "It's just a little bonus," she said as Christina opened it.

Christina felt her jaw drop when she saw the check inside. Four thousand dollars. "This is a lot of money," she protested.

"It's for the exceptional job you've done turning Gratis into a winner for me," Fredericka said with a smile.

"Thank you," Christina said hesitantly, not sure she should accept the money.

"You deserve it," Fredericka said firmly. "Are you and your family still planning to come to dinner with me tonight?" she asked, running her hand down Gratis's crooked blaze. Tired of the attention, Gratis turned away and buried his nose in his hay net.

"Of course," Christina said, still gaping at the check. "We're looking forward to it."

"I'll see you in a few hours, then," Fredericka said, and turned to go.

When she was gone, Christina settled in front of Star's stall with her racing saddle, cleaning it carefully in preparation for the next day's race. Every few minutes she touched her pocket, feeling the crackle of the envelope. She would put the money in her savings account. With her race earnings and Fredericka's generosity, maybe she really would have a chance to buy the Townsends' share of Star.

She was cleaning Star's bit with mint toothpaste when Mike and Ashleigh came looking for her. Ashleigh reached out to tuck a stray lock of Christina's reddish-brown hair behind her ear. "We need to get back to the motel and get ready for dinner," she said. "I don't think they'd let us into the restaurant with hay in our hair."

Christina quickly swept her hand over her head, feeling for stray pieces of timothy. She gave Star one last rub, then put her tack away and met her parents at the backside gate. Cindy had agreed to meet the Reeses at their motel, and had already left for her apartment in nearby Elmont to shower and change.

When Fredericka's car pulled up in front of their rooms nearly two hours later, Christina peered out the door. "Wow," she said, stepping aside so that Cindy could see the black limousine. Cindy sucked in her breath, but she didn't say anything.

"After you, my dear," Mike said in a haughty voice, and Christina giggled. The waiting chauffeur opened the passenger door for them, and Christina glanced at Ashleigh from under her eyelashes. Her mother looked as impressed as Christina felt.

"This is great," Christina said to Fredericka, who looked right at home in the car. Christina slid onto the soft leather seat and smoothed her skirt over her thighs. Cindy climbed in beside her, while Mike and Ashleigh settled onto the seat facing them.

"That shade of plum in your blouse really brings out the red highlights in your hair, Christina," Fredericka commented. Christina was glad she had taken Melanie's advice on what clothes to bring to New

York. Her own choices would definitely have been fashion blunders. She gaped out the car window as they drove toward Manhattan, overwhelmed by the amount of traffic and the constant rush of activity that seemed to be everywhere she looked.

Finally they pulled up in front of the restaurant, a low stone building with a canopy over the entry. When they walked inside, Christina glanced around the dining room, taking in the warm golds and greens of the walls and carpeting. Soft music played in the background, and the gentle clink of silver against china mingled with the quiet conversations of the other patrons. Christina recognized some of the racehorse owners and trainers, who looked a lot different here than they did at the track.

They were immediately seated at a table near a small indoor waterfall, and Christina found herself entranced by the sound of the splashing water. "I'd like to have one of those at home," she said to Cindy, who looked very elegant in a sleek black dress, her hair clipped back at the nape of her neck.

Christina traced her finger down the side of a crystal water goblet, then touched the soft linen napkin that had been folded into a pyramid.

"Ashleigh Griffen, what a pleasant surprise."

At the familiar voice, Christina turned to see Ben

al-Rihani standing near the table, a petite brunette woman at his side.

"Possibly you don't remember me," Ben said to Ashleigh. "But you haven't changed a bit. You're as lovely as you were fourteen years ago."

A broad smile brightened Ashleigh's face. "Ben al-Rihani!" she said. "Of course I remember you!"

Christina glanced at Cindy, whose face had frozen. "Ben," Ashleigh said, "you've met my husband, Mike Reese. And this is my daughter, Christina."

Ben al-Rihani nodded to Christina. "Christina and I met earlier," he said. "I should have known she was your daughter. She is quite a talented jockey, just like her mother."

"This is our friend Fredericka Graber," Ashleigh said, "and of course you know Cindy."

Ben slowly directed his gaze toward Cindy. "It's a pleasure to see you again, Cindy," he said smoothly.

"Hi, Ben," Cindy said evenly. "It's been a very long time."

"Allow me to introduce Connie Richmond," Ben said. "Connie is my head trainer."

"I see your colt Wonder's Star is racing against our colt Handsome Price tomorrow," Connie said to Ashleigh.

The trainer had all Christina's attention. If her

other colt ran like Rush Street, she and Star had better be on their toes for the race.

"The word is your colt is the horse to watch," Connie continued. She smiled at Christina. "But don't think you can outsmart my jockey two days in a row."

"I'll sure do my best," Christina responded quickly, flashing a confident smile.

Connie nodded. "And so will we."

"Will you join us for dinner?" Fredericka offered. "I'd love to hear about your horses in Dubai."

"We would love to," Ben started to say. "But—"

Christina heard Cindy's sharp intake of breath, and she turned quickly to see what had happened. Christina's fingertips struck the water goblet, but before it could spill, Cindy reached up and caught it with her left hand.

"That was close," Christina said. To her dismay, Cindy's face went white, her eyes widening with pain.

She pressed her arm close to her side and reached down to grab her bag. "I'll be right back," Cindy said, and hurried from the table.

"We made arrangements to meet some other people here," Ben continued, watching Cindy weave her way between the tables. "Perhaps we'll see you at the track tomorrow."

"I'll make sure Cindy's okay," Christina said, rising to follow Cindy through the restaurant. By the time

Christina reached the women's room, Cindy was sitting in an overstuffed chair in the lounge, her head back and her eyes closed.

"What's wrong?" Christina demanded anxiously.

"Could you get me some water?" Cindy asked, her eyes still closed. "I need to take a painkiller."

Christina filled a paper cup and handed it to Cindy. There was a prescription bottle in her hand.

"How did you hurt your arm?" Christina asked.

"Last week one of my horses banged me around pretty good while we were in the gate. I wrenched my shoulder then, on top of an old injury. The doctor gave me these"—she opened the bottle and shook out one pill—"but I don't like to take them," she said. "They're pretty strong, and a jockey without a clear head is a dangerous jockey."

"But today . . ." Christina let her voice trail off. She was going to say that Cindy had come very close to falling off in her race. Wasn't that even more dangerous?

Cindy sat up straight, glaring at Christina. "I can't just sit around and watch the races. I'll lose my edge in no time!"

"Is there anything I can do?" Christina asked, feeling uncomfortable.

"Just don't say anything, okay?" Cindy said. "I don't want everyone worrying about me."

Christina abruptly changed the subject. "Why don't you like Ben al-Rihani?" she asked.

Cindy rolled her eyes skyward. "He was a pompous jerk when I met him in Dubai," she said. "He thinks women belong in the kitchen, not in the stable."

Christina frowned in confusion. "His head trainer is a woman," she pointed out.

Cindy shrugged. "Then maybe he's changed from the arrogant little twerp I met when I was in Dubai with your mom," she said, and stood up. "Come on. Let's get back to the table before your parents and Fredericka order without us. You've got to get to bed early—you have another race to win tomorrow."

Christina followed Cindy back to the table, keeping her mind on the next day's race. She knew Star had it in him to win. But now that she had seen what kind of horses Connie Richmond trained, and after practically telling the reporter that Star was the best runner in the nation, the stakes seemed even higher. Star couldn't just win this race—he had to win it big.

3

"WE'LL SHOW THESE NEW YORK RACEHORSES JUST WHAT A Kentucky-bred colt can do, won't we, Star?" Christina said as she patted Star's glistening chestnut neck. She posted to his mincing trot as the colt followed a buckskin pony horse to the track's starting gate.

Christina sat tall on Star's back, proud to be wearing the blue-and-white silks that represented Whitebrook. She smiled confidently as they moved with the other horses in the post parade. Star followed the pony horse calmly. They were going to have a great race. She was sure of it.

"He's really easy to handle, isn't he?" the pony rider commented as Star trotted alongside the buckskin.

"Wait until he comes out of the gate," Christina

replied. "He loves to run. Besides," she added, "this is his first race at Belmont. He must know it's special. All the greatest racehorses have run here. This is his chance to show everyone he deserves to be here, too."

The beautiful Sunday afternoon weather had drawn a record crowd to the track. Christina could see her parents standing at the rail. Mike and Ashleigh were holding hands, smiling proudly as they watched her ride by. Cindy stood beside them, watching the horses intently.

Christina turned her attention back to Star. They galloped for a minute to warm up, then lined up behind the starting gate with the rest of the field.

Even though Star did better as a distance runner, Ashleigh had decided to enter him in a seven-furlong allowance race to start him out. She wanted Star and Christina to have a chance to get used to the Belmont track before they took on some longer distances.

When the pony rider handed them off to the gate crew, Star went easily into the number four chute. While they waited for the rest of the horses to be loaded, Christina settled herself on her tiny racing saddle, adjusted her goggles, and checked her helmet strap.

On either side of them, the number three and number five horses were snorting, stamping, and shifting restlessly in the narrow boxes. "Are you ready, Star?" Christina murmured. Star stood calmly, and Christina leaned forward, keeping a firm grip on the reins. "Seven furlongs, boy," she whispered. "This is a short race for you, so we need to get out in front and stay there, okay?"

Star grunted softly as if he understood her, then bobbed his head. Finally the call came that the last horse was being loaded. There was a moment of tense stillness. Christina leaned into Star's neck, ready for the race to start.

"You can do this, boy," she whispered, bracing herself. "I know you can." As she spoke, the shrill ring of the starting bell split the air and the Belmont track opened up before them.

The announcer's voice carried across the track. "And they're off!"

Star dived out of the chute, and they became part of a surging wave of horses spilling onto the track. Christina adjusted her weight over Star's pumping shoulders as the colt moved beneath her.

Belmont's dirt track was fast that day. The firm, smooth surface made running easy. Christina dropped Star to the rail with the rest of the field, pleased with how strong he felt. She envisioned Star setting a new Belmont record for a seven-furlong race. "Keep it up, Star!" she called, urging him forward.

She angled the running colt toward a small opening between the number two and number three horses.

Star's knack for running his last furlongs faster than his first ones wouldn't help him in a race this short. They needed to get out front right away.

Over the sound of the running horses' thundering hooves and snorted breaths, Christina could hear the announcer's voice ringing from the track's loud-speakers.

"Mallory has the lead, with French Sizzle a close second, and Wonder's Star is a strong third as we close on the first furlong!"

They poured down the far side of the track, heading swiftly for the only turn in the race. The race was happening too fast. Christina darted a quick glance under her arm to see the rest of the field running steadily. The number eight horse, Ben al-Rihani's colt Handsome Price, was well behind them. Christina breathed a small sigh of relief. This race would be over so fast he wouldn't have time to overtake Star.

She watched the front-runners for any sign of tiring, frustrated that there was no opening to push Star through. She didn't want to waste ground by taking him wide, but it didn't look as though she was going to have much choice.

Just as they reached the third pole, Christina could see the number seven horse moving up to their right, blocking the outside.

"It's Mallory holding the lead, with French Sizzle a

strong second, but Final Twist is coming up on the outside to pass Wonder's Star as we go into the fourth furlong!"

Christina took another quick glance behind her. The rest of the horses seemed to be holding their positions easily. "We don't have time to wait, boy," she said urgently. The colt flicked his ears at the sound of her voice, then dug into the track. Ahead of them the number three and number seven horses ran strong, but Christina could see French Sizzle, the number two horse, on the rail, start to falter.

She pushed Star, but it seemed to be taking all his strength just to hold his position. Christina felt a tinge of fear course through her. Star should be running easily right now, boxed in or not, but he didn't feel right under her. She fought down a pang of worry, trying to concentrate on the race.

"French Sizzle is losing ground," the announcer called. "Number eight, Handsome Price, is pulling up on the inside, overtaking Wonder's Star."

Christina could hear the rhythmic pounding of Handsome Price's hooves, but the challenger was a blur of chestnut and black-and-silver silks at the corner of her eye. She focused her sights between Star's ears, searching for a chance to move him into the front.

They shot past the fourth pole, neck and neck with the number eight horse. Then the number seven horse,

Final Twist, veered right, and a sliver of space opened up ahead of them.

Christina adjusted her grip on Star's reins and leaned forward. "Go!" she yelled. "Come on, Star, move!" She felt the colt's muscles bunch with effort. But the three leaders held their places, and to her left the number eight horse, Handsome Price, suddenly shot through the gap between Star and the rail.

Star seemed offended by the bold move, and he redoubled his efforts. But in spite of the push, his strides began to feel heavy and his breathing sounded labored. His movements were strained, as though he were running in mud, not on a fast track. Christina choked back a sob of frustration as the rest of the field poured around them.

"Wonder's Star is out of it!" the announcer called. "Time is running out, and Handsome Price is giving an eye-catching performance as he continues to close on the leaders."

"Come on, Star," Christina pleaded, urging the laboring colt forward. "Just two more furlongs. I know you can do this! Come on, boy!"

Star flicked his ears in response to Christina's voice, and as they bore down on the sixth pole, he seemed to snap out of his doldrums. He rallied, stretching his neck and extending his legs, putting his heart into every stride.

"Wonder's Star is making a move now," the announcer exclaimed. "They don't have far to go, but it looks like the Whitebrook colt might pull it off!"

Christina felt her heart soar as Star ran magnificently, closing on the leaders to regain the ground he had lost.

"We're going to do it, boy!" she cried. But as they neared the end of the race Star's surge of speed took its toll. Christina could feel the tremendous effort he put into each step, just to cross the finish line.

"And at the finish it's Handsome Price, followed by Mallory and French Sizzle!"

Christina and Star ended the race an unimpressive seventh in a field of ten. Star didn't even fight to keep going, the way he usually did when Christina brought him back down to a trot.

Mike and Ashleigh met her on the track as she leaped from the exhausted colt's back. Star hung his head, breathing hard, his neck lathered from exertion. Dani ran out to take his saddle and pads while Ashleigh felt Star's heaving chest. Mike draped his arm over Christina's shoulders as she fought back a sob of worry.

"Let's walk him out," Ashleigh said, eyeing Star anxiously. "I don't know what happened to the two of you out there. You looked great at the start. He just didn't seem to have any staying power today."

"There's something the matter with him!" Christina fretted, walking beside her mother as Ashleigh led Star from the track. "He felt so wrong out there, Mom. He tried harder than I've ever felt him run, but he just couldn't keep it up." Christina noticed Cindy watching them from the rail.

"We'll have the track vet look him over," Ashleigh said, shaking her head. She patted Star's sweating shoulder. "You certainly didn't give the race away, did you, boy? You looked like you were trying your hardest."

"He was!" Christina exclaimed. "He put everything he had into it, Mom."

As they reached the backside Dani returned with Star's cooling sheet. Ashleigh draped it over the colt while Christina held his head. "I wish you could talk," she said, rubbing the star on the colt's forehead with her fingertips. "Don't you feel well, boy?"

In response, Star nudged her with his nose. His eyes were bright and clear, but he was trembling and sweat-soaked, and his breathing was still labored.

"Let Dani walk him while you get out of your silks, Chris," Ashleigh said.

Christina shook her head. "I'm staying with Star," she said stubbornly.

Ashleigh paused, then nodded. "Okay. We'll see you back at his stall."

"I'll go clean your tack and put some extra bedding

in his stall," Dani said, heading after Ashleigh and Mike.

Christina walked Star around the barns toward the back paddock. The flurry of race-time activity around the backside seemed to be happening somewhere way in the distance. Her attention was completely centered on the chestnut colt at her side.

Christina paused to check Star's body heat every couple of minutes and to offer him a little water. Before long he was dry and breathing easily. Christina led him toward the wash rack.

Dani met her there, a bucket of soapy water and a wash mitt in her hand. "He looks good right now," the groom said. "Maybe he just had a bad race."

"Maybe," Christina said doubtfully. But she knew better. Star hadn't had a bad race since he started racing. When he hadn't won, it had been a riding error. Something was definitely wrong with him.

"You need to change," Dani said. "I'll give him his bath and get him back to the stall. Your mom said the vet will be by soon."

Christina raced back to the locker room and quickly changed her clothes, leaving her hair in the tight braid she had worn under her riding helmet. By the time she returned to Star's stall, Ashleigh was holding the colt steady while the track vet scoped his air passages.

Seeing the long tube threaded up Star's nostril made Christina cringe, but the colt didn't seem to be bothered by the examination. She stood at his shoulder, stroking his neck and murmuring reassurances to him.

In a minute the vet stepped back, shaking his head. "His lungs are clear," he said. "He definitely didn't bleed." As he talked, he pulled out a large syringe and proceeded to draw blood from Star, bringing another sympathetic shudder from Christina.

"That's good for two apples, boy," she said, gently rubbing his poll.

"I have to say he looks fine right now," the vet said, holding up the vial of blood. "We'll run some tests and see if we can identify anything, but I'm afraid your horse may just have had an off day on the track." He gave Christina a reassuring smile, then picked up his bag.

Christina forced a smile in response. "Thank you," she said, turning to Star as the vet walked away. "Do you think we should still keep him in the Champagne?" Christina asked Ashleigh, stroking Star's smooth coat. In two weeks, the colt was entered to run in Belmont's Champagne Stakes, an important race for two-year-olds. But after that day's lackluster performance, Ashleigh might decide to scratch Star from the prestigious race.

"Of course he's still running," Ashleigh said. "Right now you need to take care of his legs. Your dad is in Vince's office, calling Whitebrook to tell everyone about Star's race."

Christina nodded, picking up the bucket of leg wraps and liniment. She went into Star's stall while her mother headed across the aisle to Vince's office.

The people who worked at Whitebrook were more like extended family than farm employees. Cindy's adoptive father, Ian McLean, his wife, Beth, and their son, Kevin, lived in a cottage at the farm. Ian had been working for Mike and Ashleigh as the farm's head trainer long before Christina had even been born.

Dani mixed a hot mash for Star while Christina rubbed his legs down with liniment. She carefully bandaged each one while the colt worked on his pan of feed. Christina was pleased to see that he ate eagerly. "You're all right, aren't you, boy?" she asked, running her hand down his neck. Maybe Star *had* just had a bad race. She cringed inwardly as she recalled the way she had bragged about him to the reporter. But in her heart she knew Star was no slacker. There had to be something wrong with Star for him to have performed so badly. But outwardly the colt showed no signs of trouble, and Christina couldn't imagine what the problem might have been.

"I'll put this stuff away," Dani said, picking up the

grooming supplies and heading out of the stall.

Christina leaned her head on Star's shoulder, feeling the warmth radiate from him. The colt brought his head around and rested it against her, and for several minutes they stood together quietly. She rubbed his shoulder, feeling the powerful muscles rippling under his smooth, glossy coat. Star pressed his nose against her arm, scratching his muzzle on the seam of her jacket.

"Does that feel good, silly?" she asked, pulling his forelock playfully. Finally she checked that his blanket was in place and made sure his water bucket was full.

"I'll be back to see you in a bit," she said, stroking his nose. "I still need to find you those apples I promised."

She stepped out of the stall, relieved to see how much better Star looked now. But when she latched the door, she glanced back inside. Star had moved to the back of the stall, and she could barely see him. His head was hanging low as he stood motionless in the shadows.

"EVERYTHING ALL SET TO GO?" ASHLEIGH ASKED, PUTTING her travel bag down on the floor by Christina's bed. Mike sat at the hotel room's desk, the phone receiver pressed to his ear.

Christina nodded at her mother, wrinkling her nose. "Everything except Star," she said. "I don't think I should leave, Mom. I know there's something wrong with him. I should stay here for him."

Ashleigh sighed. "I understand how you feel, Chris. But I'm sure he's fine. Dani will take good care of him, and the track vet will check on him every day."

"And you'll be back next weekend," Mike said, hanging up the phone. "Cindy is meeting us at the airport," he added. "She got a ticket on our flight."

Ashleigh and Mike had convinced Cindy to stay at

49

Whitebrook while her shoulder healed.

"Ian and Beth are going to be so thrilled to see her," Ashleigh said happily.

A horn blared outside the motel, and Mike glanced out the window. "That's our cab," he said. "Let's get going."

Cindy's seat on the plane was several rows away from the Reeses. Christina glanced around after they had reached altitude to see Cindy slip a pair of headphones on and lean back with her eyes closed. *So much for visiting with her,* Christina thought, turning around. Her parents were reading copies of *Bloodhorse* and *Backstretch.* Mike offered her a copy of the *Daily Racing Form.*

Christina left the paper unopened on her lap and stared out at the clouds beneath the plane, her mind on Star. *I'll be back in five days,* she kept reminding herself. And after the Champagne Stakes he'd be coming home. But she still was sure something was wrong with Star, even if no one else could see it. The thought of him so far from her gnawed at her the entire flight home.

Ian McLean was waiting for them at Bluegrass Airport. When they came into the terminal, Christina saw the red-haired trainer's welcoming smile change to a look of shocked happiness when he saw Cindy. He blinked, shook his head, then stepped forward, holding his arms out to his adopted daughter.

"Hi, Dad," Cindy said, her voice muffled as Ian enveloped her in an enthusiastic hug.

"This is such a wonderful surprise," Ian said, stepping back and holding Cindy at arm's length. "I can't believe you're here!"

"I don't know how long I'm staying," Cindy said quickly. "I should have called first, but it was all sort of last-minute." Christina didn't miss the sharp look Cindy gave Ashleigh. "I'm taking a few weeks off to heal up a bit, and Ashleigh and Mike insisted I come home with them." She smiled thinly. "So here I am."

"I'm glad to see you no matter what the reason!" Ian exclaimed, keeping his arm draped over Cindy's shoulders as they headed for the baggage claim. "Is it the left shoulder that's bothering you again?"

Cindy sighed. "Yeah—the same one I keep injuring," she said.

"Beth will help you find a good doctor," Ian said. "She knows about the good ones from her exercise classes." He picked up Cindy's suitcase and led the way out to the car. "Beth is going to be so excited to see you," he said.

"It'll be good to see her and Kevin, too," Cindy said. But it seemed to Christina that Cindy was less than happy to be home.

Cindy sat beside Christina in the backseat for the

drive home. Christina gazed out the window, enjoying the familiar sights, while Ian filled Mike and Ashleigh in on the daily activities at Whitebrook.

"It hasn't changed much since I left," Cindy commented as they passed white-fenced bluegrass pastures and farms of all sizes. Some had large, elegant barns, with huge signs at the gates boasting of their horses' bloodlines, while others had smaller, simple outbuildings and plain wooden fences.

Christina preferred this peaceful scenery to the intense, busy sights of New York. She sighed, her contentment shadowed by the knowledge that Star was still there. Even though Dani was there to take care of him, Christina felt horrible for leaving him.

"This is going to take some getting used to," Cindy said. "It's so quiet."

"Much nicer than New York," Christina said.

Cindy shot her an amused look. "You get used to the pace," she said.

Christina shook her head. "Never," she replied. "I like it here best."

When they turned up the drive into Whitebrook, Cindy craned her neck left and right, trying to see everything. "The place looks great," she said.

Christina looked around the farm, trying to see it as Cindy would after being away for so many years. The sun had almost set, casting shadows on the white board fencing that lined the driveway, and on the main farm-house, where a light gleamed from the kitchen window. The lights were on in the barns, too, where Jonnie and Joe, two of Whitebrook's grooms, were doing the evening chores. Christina could see George Ballard's car parked by the stallion barn. Whitebrook's stallion manager always stayed late in the evening to be sure the stallions were taken care of to his exacting stan-dards.

"You'll be able to see it better tomorrow," Ashleigh said, twisting around in the front seat. "It hasn't changed a lot since you left."

Cindy smiled. "I guess I'm glad you talked me into this, Ash," she said. "I needed a vacation."

Christina frowned. Being ordered not to race didn't sound like a vacation to her, but maybe after so many years of riding, it did to Cindy.

Ian dropped the Reeses off in front of the old white farmhouse, then he and Cindy headed for the McLeans' cottage.

Christina heaved her bag onto her shoulder and followed her parents into the house. Melanie was at the sink, deftly slicing carrots into small pieces. "Wel-come home," she said, grinning happily. "Dinner will be served in about half an hour."

"Hi, Mel," Ashleigh said, crossing the room to give Melanie a hug.

Mike sniffed the air. "What are you cooking? It smells great."

Melanie cocked an eyebrow. "You might want to take that back, Uncle Mike. It's stir-fried tofu."

Christina giggled. "I'm so hungry I'll eat anything," she said to her cousin. She shifted her heavy bag onto her other shoulder. "But I need to sort out my laundry first."

"I'll come help you," Melanie said, taking the big frying pan off the stove. "This stuff can sit for a while." She followed Christina upstairs.

While Christina emptied her suitcase, Melanie sat on her bed, her knees pulled to her chest. "Who was in the car with Ian?" she asked, eyeing Christina curiously.

Christina quickly told her about Cindy. "She sure didn't seem very happy about leaving the track," she said

"It would be awful to hurt yourself so badly you couldn't ride anymore," Melanie said, shuddering dramatically. "I don't know what I'd do."

"Well, Cindy is only off the track for a little while. She just needs some time for her shoulder to recuperate."

Melanie shrugged. "Whatever," she said. "I'm just glad she's here. Can we go over after dinner so you can introduce me?"

"Sure," Christina said, opening her bag. "I can't believe I got so many clothes dirty in just two days," she commented, tossing item after item into a laundry basket.

"Imagine living out of a suitcase and following the racing circuit," Melanie said. "You'd have to go to the laundromat all the time."

"I think I'd rather stick around here and ride from home," Christina said firmly. "Life on the road doesn't sound like fun at all."

"It does to me," Melanie said. "I'd love to travel around, riding in different states and seeing different places."

"Make sure you have at least some races on the East Coast," Christina said. "I don't want to have to fly all the way across the country to visit you."

"No problem," Melanie replied agreeably. She leaned forward, examining the stack of books Christina had just placed on her desk. "Chris, did you actually study your driver ed manual this weekend?" she asked jokingly. Melanie wasn't exactly diligent about her schoolwork.

"I studied on the plane Friday afternoon," Christina said. "I think I'm ready for the test tomorrow."

"Test?" Melanie jumped to her feet. "I forgot about that! Can I borrow your book?" She took it before Christina could even nod. "I'd better study before I eat any dinner."

After starting her laundry, Christina went to her parents' office to use the phone. When she dialed the Townsends' number, a strange voice answered the phone.

"Townsend residence," a woman said formally.

"I'm calling for Parker," Christina said politely.

"Mr. Parker is not available" the maid replied.

"Do you know if he's at Whisperwood?" Christina asked, referring to the nearby training facility owned by Ian McLean's elder daughter, Samantha, and her husband, Tor Nelson. Parker kept his event horse at Whisperwood and worked part-time for the Nelsons, giving riding lessons.

"I don't know, ma'am," the maid said.

The brief conversation made Christina grateful for the casual way her family lived. She wouldn't trade having to help with all the work at Whitebrook for the Townsends' stiff, formal lifestyle. Even though he was a Townsend, Parker didn't fit in well with Brad and Lavinia's upscale lives, either. That was one reason he and Christina got along so well.

Christina left a message for her boyfriend, then wandered into the kitchen. Her father was putting the finishing touches on a salad. Mike pointed at the forks and spoons sitting on the counter. "You can set the table," he told Christina.

"Where's Mom?" she asked, picking up the flat-ware.

"Take a guess," Mike said with a laugh.

"The barn?" Christina asked, although she already knew the answer.

Just then the door opened and Ashleigh came into the house. "Everything looks good in the barns," she said. "And the vet from Belmont called while I was in the office."

"Is Star all right?" Christina demanded, dropping the silverware on the table.

"They couldn't find anything in the blood work they did," Ashleigh said. "But the vet promised to keep a close eye on him."

"I hope he's okay this week," Christina said, arranging the flatware at each place. "I'm still worried."

"I'm sure he's fine," Ashleigh reassured her. "And the week will go by fast."

After dinner, Melanie and Christina did the dishes, then headed for the McLeans' cottage. Beth met them at the door. "Cindy went to bed early," she said. "But I know she'll be happy to see you two tomorrow. I'm sure she'll be at the barn first thing in the morning."

Christina didn't mind. The weekend had been long and exhausting. She was happy to go to bed.

Christina slept well in her own bed, and the next morning she awoke early, pulled on jeans and a sweatshirt, and headed for the barn. Before school she and Melanie always helped with the morning chores and exercised some of the fillies and colts in training.

Melanie was already on the track, riding Rascal, one of Whitebrook's three-year-olds. The sun was peeking over the horizon, and Joe and Jonnie were leading the broodmares out to their turnouts for the day.

"Where's Ian?" Christina asked Maureen Mack, the assistant trainer, who was holding Catwink, a gray two-year-old filly. Catwink inhaled loudly, taking up Christina's scent, and Christina paused to stroke the filly's dappled shoulder.

"He's running late this morning," Maureen said, giving Christina a leg up onto the gray horse's back. "He and Beth wanted to spend some time with Cindy." She patted Catwink's neck while Christina adjusted her stirrups and picked up the reins.

"Just a regular workout today," Maureen said, stepping back so that Christina could head the filly onto the exercise track.

She met up with Melanie, and they jogged the Thoroughbreds side by side, their breath puffing faintly in the early morning air. Mist rose from the sprawling fields of bluegrass, and patches of yellow and red dotted the trees.

"We need to go for a ride," Melanie said. "It feels like forever since we've been on the trails."

"Sounds good to me," Christina said, posting easily to Catwink's gait. "Maybe after school? Parker is supposed to be working for Sam. We could ride over to Whisperwood and watch him teach a class."

"Sure," Melanie said, keeping a tight rein on Rascal, who rolled his eyes and crow-hopped a few steps. She got him settled down quickly. "Maybe we could get Cindy to go with us. I have about a million questions I want to ask her."

After they had finished working their horses Christina stopped by the barn office before she returned to the house to get ready for school. Ashleigh was at the desk, looking through a file folder.

"Have you heard anything from Belmont?" Christina asked from the doorway.

Ashleigh glanced up. "I talked to the track vet again," she said. "So far Star seems fine. The colt in the stall next to him is off his feed, though."

"Fire 'n' Ice," Christina said. "He didn't look very good when I saw him on Saturday." She filled her mother in on her conversation with the colt's groom.

Ashleigh frowned. "I'll put in another call to the

vet and see what they know about him," she promised. "You'd better get changed. Your dad is waiting to drive you and Mel to class."

"Thanks, Mom," Christina said. She was reluctant to leave without knowing more, but she was aware that arguing with her mother wouldn't do her any good.

After her morning classes, Christina ate lunch with Katie Garrity and Melanie. Katie was wearing a pink T-shirt that advertised the school's production of the musical *Grease*.

"I can't believe how much work goes into putting on a musical," Katie said. "I have rehearsals every day after school for hours. And all for two performances."

Christina smiled distractedly, her thoughts still on Star. Maybe she had time before her next class to call home and see if there was any news from Belmont.

"Kind of like horse racing," Melanie said. "You spend weeks conditioning your horse for a two-minute race."

Katie laughed. "Leave it to you to compare acting to horse racing," she said.

Christina rose. "I'll see you in driver ed," she said, and headed for the pay phone. Maureen answered the phone at the barn office. There had been no news from New York, so Christina went to her next class, trying to tell herself that no news was good news.

Driver education was the last class of the day. Mr. Hamrick passed out copies of a test on the rules of the road. Christina glanced at the questions, then looked up at Melanie, who was sitting in the next aisle. Melanie caught her gaze and grinned. *So easy*, she mouthed, and Christina had to stifle a giggle.

She and Melanie sat together on the bus on the ride home. "I always thought when I got my driver's license my first car would be a fancy sports car," Melanie said.

Christina glanced over at her cousin. "But now you're thinking a full-size pickup would be nice because you could pull a horse trailer."

Melanie laughed out loud. "You read my mind," she said.

When they arrived at Whitebrook, they walked up the long drive, heading for the house.

"We still have time to go for a ride before dinner," Melanie suggested.

"Let's get changed and go, then," Christina said, eager to take a brisk ride through the woods. "If you want to ride Rascal, I'll take Sassy Jazz."

"You're on," Melanie said, picking up her pace.

But as they started past the main barn, Christina saw a shiny, low-slung sports car parked near the barn door.

"There's my car," Melanie said, laughing. "It was nice of them to deliver it for me."

A smart reply died in Christina's throat as she recognized one of Brad Townsend's many cars. "I'm going to go see what my favorite person is doing here," she said warily.

"I'll take your books," Melanie offered, reaching out for Christina's book bag.

Christina gritted her teeth and headed for the barn, the trail ride forgotten.

Whatever Brad wanted, it had something to do with Star.

5

WHEN SHE NEARED THE OFFICE DOOR, CHRISTINA COULD hear Brad's voice, his words clipped and his tone demanding. She stopped as abruptly as though she had walked into a wall.

"I'd like to know exactly what happened yesterday," Brad said. "Seventh place is inexcusable." Brad stood in the office doorway with his back to Christina. Even from behind he looked imposing, dressed in a tweed sports jacket and beige slacks, his fisted hand propped on his hip.

Christina caught a glimpse of her mother sitting at her desk, her fingers steepled under her chin, her face composed as she gazed up at Brad.

"Star had a bad race," Ashleigh said calmly. "It's

bound to happen, Brad. You know perfectly well that losing races is a part of this business."

"Not when Townsend Acres is involved!" Brad said forcefully. "If Christina had been paying attention during the race, she wouldn't have missed at least a dozen chances to get Star out in front. She got over-confident, and she blew it."

Christina gritted her teeth. Cindy had said the same thing about being too confident, but Christina knew she'd been totally focused. Brad was wrong. She hadn't blown the race, and Star had run his heart out.

"Please don't blame Chris," Ashleigh said neutrally. "She works better with Star than anyone else. She certainly wouldn't have let him down. Star had an off day. Let it go, Brad. "

Christina admired the even tone of her mother's voice. It took all the self-control she had not to step forward and give Brad a piece of her own mind.

Brad waved a newspaper in the air, his face red with anger. "According to sportswriter Randy Neff, Christina has tremendous confidence in Star. Apparently she's riding him in the Derby in May, whether we want her to or not!"

Brad's sarcastic tone had Christina drawing back a little. She'd forgotten about the reporter.

"What business does Christina have giving interviews to the press about Star's races?" Brad demanded angrily. "She has no ownership in that colt."

"I don't know what you're talking about," Ashleigh said slowly, dropping her hands, palms down, on the desk.

"Read this," Brad said, stepping forward to shove the paper across the desk. "Christina would do well to remember that she is merely Star's jockey. Where does she get off saying that Star's a sure thing for the Kentucky Derby? As far as I know, we haven't entered him in any of the Championship series races. It seems to me that something so important should be a joint decision, Ashleigh. And the press release should be something Star's owners agree on."

Christina wanted to shrivel up and disappear. Randy must have put every word she said into his article. She took a cautious step back, not so sure she wanted to face Brad now.

Ashleigh exhaled loudly, obviously upset. "I'll talk to Chris," she said. "It won't happen again."

"It had better not," Brad said. "I don't want to see any more statements like that in print. Your daughter had no business even talking to a reporter on her own."

"I told you we'd take care of it, Brad," Ashleigh said sharply.

"Good," Brad said. "There's one other thing," he added, dropping his voice to a softer pitch and shifting so that his shoulder was resting against the door jamb.

Christina stiffened at the change in his tone and his pose. Brad was never nice unless he wanted something. The sudden change in his demeanor worried her more than his anger.

"What is it?" Ashleigh asked, rising and coming around the desk. She propped herself on the edge of the desk and folded her arms in front of her.

"I want to bring Star back to Townsend Acres."

Christina felt as if the barn were spinning around her. He couldn't! Her mother would never let that happen. Not after what Star had gone through as a yearling there, when the sensitive colt suffered under the handling of Brad's head trainer, Ralph Dunkirk. Going back to the Townsends' farm would be the worst thing in the world for Star.

Christina clenched her fists and took a step forward, prepared to face Brad in order to defend Star.

But before she could say anything, she saw Ashleigh shake her head. "I don't think that's a good idea, Brad," she said. "Star didn't do well there, and you know it. Since we've had him here and Chris has been handling him, the colt's come around completely."

"As she so aptly proved over the weekend?" Brad commented icily. "It will be different this time if you bring him back to Townsend Acres," he added, his voice low and calm. "Star isn't a foal anymore. He can handle Ralph's training."

Christina shuddered involuntarily at the sound of Brad's attempt at sweet-talking.

"Ralph and I agree that Star has Derby potential," Brad continued. "But I'm still very concerned about Saturday's disappointing performance."

"That has nothing to do with his training here," Ashleigh said quickly.

"You don't have the facilities that we have," Brad said. "Townsend Acres has the best conditioning equipment available, Ashleigh. You can still oversee his training," he continued, his voice remaining pleasant. "And Christina can continue to jockey him and work with him. You can pick his groom.

"Think about it, Ashleigh. The Townsend facility is one of the finest in the area. Everything Star needs to bring him into top condition is there. It's what's best for the colt. Besides," he added, raising his eyebrows, "think of the status another Derby winner would bring to both our farms."

Terrified that Brad's sales pitch was lulling her mother into agreement, Christina stepped forward and squeezed past Brad into the office. "You're not taking Star!" she said adamantly. If Star went to Townsend Acres, she'd never get the colt back again.

And she'd lose all hope of buying Brad's share in him. The thought made her legs go weak.

Brad glared down at her, his eyes glinting fiercely. "You don't have a say in this, Christina," he thundered. "You're the colt's jockey, not his owner. This is a business arrangement. We're not talking about a pet pony here. We have to maximize Star's potential."

"I won't let you take him," Christina insisted desperately. "I'll buy your share in him."

Brad's eyes widened and an amused smirk tugged at his lips. "You'll buy him?" he repeated, rolling his eyes. "With what? Be realistic, Christina. Even if you could afford him, which you can't, Townsend Acres' interest in Star isn't for sale."

Christina felt her dream of owning Star collapsing. *As if it had ever been a possibility anyway,* she reminded herself bitterly. The most she could hope for was that Star would stay at Whitebrook.

"He doesn't need your fancy equipment," she said, looking at Brad steadily. "He needs me."

"Don't you know what it would mean to Townsend Acres and to Whitebrook if Star swept the Triple Crown?" Brad asked. "Just winning the Derby would increase his stud fees dramatically."

It was obvious that Brad cared nothing for Star's well-being. He was only interested in money and the status a Derby-winning colt could bring to Townsend Acres.

"You're not taking Star," Christina repeated firmly.

"That's right," Ashleigh said quickly. "I agree with Chris. We're not going to hand him over at this point, Brad. We've put too much hard work into him, and I don't think we've done too badly, either."

"Then you need someone to work with you on his conditioning," Brad argued. "If he can't perform well in a little allowance race, how is he going to compete in the Champagne or the races beyond that?"

"We'll get his schedule worked out," Ashleigh said, her tone signaling that she was not going to be pushed around.

"Just remember," Brad said, glowering at Christina. "Your daughter is his jockey, and nothing more. If he puts in another disgraceful performance like he did on Saturday, we will find a replacement for her. I want you to breeze him before the Champagne Stakes, and I want to be consulted about his time. If she can't get him to run well, then she's a liability. I won't have it."

Ashleigh narrowed her eyes. "Fine," she replied coolly.

"And remember, Ashleigh," Brad continued, "you only own half of Wonder's Star. I will not throw away my shot at a Triple Crown winner because Christina has a soft spot for the colt. He needs the best training we can provide for him."

Ashleigh's eyes widened. "Are you saying I'm not

a capable trainer, Brad? It seems to me old Charlie Burke and I did fine without any special equipment when we trained Wonder."

When Brad remained silent, Christina knew her mother had struck a nerve.

Ashleigh stood tall, glaring up at Brad. "We can manage his training without your interference. Star will be more than ready for the Champagne Stakes."

"Have it your way," Brad said. "But if he doesn't end up in the money . . ." He paused and looked from Ashleigh to Christina. "We will have this discussion again, and I promise you I won't back down." He spun on his heel and strode away, leaving Christina and Ashleigh alone.

Brad's footsteps faded down the aisle, and Christina released a pent-up breath. "Thanks for standing up for Star, Mom," she said, feeling her shoulders sag as she heard Brad's car engine roar to life.

Ashleigh sighed. "Brad can be very annoying," she said, then laughed at the look Christina shot her. "Okay," she said. "That was an understatement. Brad is a royal pain. He gets to me, too. But we still have to tolerate him." Ashleigh picked up the newspaper and held it out to Christina with a frown. "When did you talk to a reporter?"

"Saturday," Christina said, her face growing hot. She filled her mother in on the conversation in front of the jockeys' lounge. "He just got me so mad, Mom," she said. "I couldn't let him say such awful things about Star."

Ashleigh sighed. "Well, the damage is done," she said, and handed Christina the paper.

Christina sank onto a chair and ran her fingertip over the headline of the sports section of the New York paper.

"Has Wonder's Star Burned Out?" the headline read in big, bold print. Christina ground her teeth as she read the article, which included a terrible photo of Star right after the race, when Ashleigh and Mike had rushed out to meet her on the track. Star's head was down and his legs were splayed. The picture made Christina want to cry. Star looked totally defeated.

The reporter had listed Star's wins, then suggested that the colt had peaked during the summer and was now a has-been.

"Star's jockey, Christina Reese, guaranteed that the colt will be in the starting gate at next May's Kentucky Derby," the article read. "But from his performance on Sunday, it is clear that Wonder's Star is destined to be a Derby dropout."

"One lousy race," Christina fumed, "and this guy says Star should be put out to pasture. He doesn't know anything!"

She felt the heat rise in her face as she read her own words, twisted into a meaning she had never intended.

71

"This is the last time I ever talk to a media person," she vowed, crumpling the paper into an untidy ball. She jumped from her chair "I'm sorry about the article," she said to Ashleigh. "That reporter made me sound like I was bragging about a loser horse, and I wasn't. Star's not a loser."

Ashleigh nodded with a wry smile. "I know," she said. "It's hard not to let your heart take over when someone is talking down a horse you love." She gave Christina's shoulder a light squeeze. "I'm sure you'll think before you say anything to a reporter after this."

"I will, believe me," Christina said. "So, have you heard anything more about how Star's doing? Has the vet said anything?" she asked.

"Dani called earlier," Ashleigh said. "Star is still eating and he seems to be fine."

"What about that horse in the other stall?" Christina asked, unconvinced that everything was all right. As much as she hated the thought that Star might be ill, she still couldn't believe his poor showing in the race was his fault. Or hers.

"They moved him to the vet barn," Ashleigh said. "So far they haven't been able to identify what's wrong with him, but they're still running tests."

Christina pursed her lips. "Maybe I should go back up to Belmont before the weekend," she said worriedly.

Ashleigh shook her head. "There's nothing you can do, Chris. Maureen is heading up there this afternoon to oversee his works until the Champagne, and Dani is with him all the time. Star is in good hands. You know that."

Christina nodded reluctantly. "Yes," she said, "but I'll still feel much better when he's home again."

"I know," Ashleigh said, then looked past Christina to the office doorway. "Hi there," she said, smiling warmly.

Christina turned to see Cindy standing in the doorway. "I was just looking for Ian," Cindy said. "Have you seen him?"

Ashleigh nodded. "He's at the stallion barn with Mike and George."

Cindy started to turn away.

"I'll walk over there with you," Christina said quickly. She fell into step beside Cindy. "How's your shoulder?" she asked.

"It's fine," Cindy said, dismissing the subject with a sharp gesture. "I'll be back on the track soon."

Christina glanced at Cindy, dismayed to see her scowling deeply. "Did you see a doctor yet?" Christina asked, surprised.

"No," Cindy said. "I have an appointment with a specialist tomorrow. But I'm sure he'll okay me to race. I don't think the track doctor knew what he was talking about when he told me not to ride."

"I have a question I've been meaning to ask you, since you've been in so many races," Christina said as they neared the stallion barn. "You know how sometimes when you come out of the gate, you can feel your horse start to—"

"I don't want to talk about it, Chris," Cindy said curtly, speeding up.

"But I wasn't asking about your shoulder," Christina protested. "I just wanted—"

"I don't want to talk about racing, period," Cindy said through gritted teeth.

"Fine," Christina said, hurt and perplexed by Cindy's rudeness.

"It doesn't look like the stallion barn has changed much," Cindy said, abruptly changing the subject.

Christina felt her shoulders sag. Cindy wasn't exactly an easy person to get to know. And Christina was starting to wonder if she *wanted* to know her. She could be so bristly.

When they stepped inside the door to the stallion barn, Christina could hear her father talking to George Ballard, the stallion manager.

"I'm looking forward to having this building upgraded and expanded," George was saying. Christina could see Ian standing beside Mike, both men towering over the stockily built, gray-haired stallion manager. The three of them were gazing at a sheet of paper taped to the barn wall.

"Hey there, Jazzman." Cindy stopped near the old stallion's stall. "Long time no see, old man."

Christina stood beside Cindy and admired the big black horse. Jazzman had sired Star, along with several other successful racehorses, including Sassy Jazz, the mare Christina had ridden to get her apprentice license.

Jazzman flared his nostrils, taking in their scents. Christina held her hand flat so he could snuffle it. "Star got a lot of his personality from you, didn't he, fellow?" she said, tickling the soft edge of his nose with her fingertips.

"Jazzman was here when I came to Whitebrook." Cindy said, looking the stallion over. "He still looks pretty fit."

Christina examined the stallion. Jazzman was indeed regal and powerful, in spite of his age.

She noticed that though Cindy spoke fondly of the elegant stallion, she didn't touch him or the stallion next to him, Blues King, another of Whitebrook's older stallions, who nickered a greeting at them. Christina gave Blues King an affectionate pat. "I'll bring you a carrot later," she promised him.

Cindy glanced at her disapprovingly. "They're racehorses, not puppies, Chris," she said. "You don't have to treat them like pets."

Christina pressed her lips together, biting back a tart response. Cindy was a visitor, she reminded herself. She knew that giving the horses a little extra attention didn't hurt anything. Cindy was so cold and matter-of-fact, Christina bet she rarely gave a horse even a quick pat after a race. Christina couldn't imagine never petting Star or talking to him the way she always did.

There was an empty stall between Blues King and the next stallion, Terminator. The big black horse pinned his ears and snaked his neck threateningly as Cindy and Christina passed near him. Christina made a face at the aggressive stallion and stepped farther into the aisle, closer to the stalls across the aisle, where Saturday Affair, Make It So, Wonder's Pride, and March to Glory were stabled.

"Hey, Pride," she said, rubbing the chestnut stallion's nose lightly.

"He looks great," Cindy commented without pausing as she headed purposefully to where Mike, Ian, and George stood talking.

Mike smiled at Christina and gestured at a piece of paper in his hand. It was a blueprint. "Our barn remodeling," he said proudly. "We're adding more stalls. After next year, Star will be in here too. I'm looking forward to the expansion. It's going to be top-notch."

George Ballard nodded firmly. George had handled Whitebrook's stallions for years and had a brisk, no-

nonsense quality about him, but Christina saw an excited gleam in his eye. "The contractor will be here tomorrow to review the details, and construction starts next week. The addition should be done by November."

Cindy turned to Ian. "I need to talk to you," she said bluntly.

Christina stiffened at Cindy's tone of voice. It was clear she had no interest in the expansion of the stallion barn, even though it was part of her own father's work. Ian was one of the nicest people Christina knew. Even if Cindy was his daughter, she had no business being so rude.

"That's great about the barn," Christina said to George and her father as Cindy and Ian walked away. She glanced at her watch. It was too late now to tack up for a trail ride. She hoped Melanie wouldn't be too disappointed.

"I'd better get over to the mares' barn," she said. "I have chores to do before I get started on my homework."

She left the barn, her thoughts on Cindy and Star. Maybe Cindy's arm was a lot worse than she let on, and that was what was troubling her. But if Christina had her way, Cindy and Star would switch places. All she wanted was for Star to come home, and then things would get back to normal.

6

ON TUESDAY MORNING BEFORE SCHOOL CHRISTINA STOPPED by the barn office, where her mother was already going over the day's schedule with Ian.

"Have you called Belmont yet?" Christina asked, anxious to hear any news about Star. "Is Maureen there yet?"

Ashleigh nodded. "I called. Maureen says Star is doing all right, but he's still a little droopy. The vet isn't in yet, but the assistant at the clinic said they've quarantined Fire 'n' Ice."

"What does he have?" Christina demanded anxiously. "Is it contagious?"

"They still don't know," Ashleigh said calmly. "They moved him to the isolation barn as a precaution. I'm sure it isn't anything, Chris," she added reassur-

78

ingly. "All the horses at the track had clean vet checks."

Unless it was something they didn't know to test for, Christina thought, her stomach turning with worry.

"I'll let you know right away if we hear anything," Ashleigh promised. "You'd better get out to the track. Jonnie has Missy waiting for you."

Christina turned away reluctantly and started down the aisle. She saw Cindy standing in front of Sassy Jazz's stall, her arms folded in front of her.

"I didn't come home to take a job as a groom!" Cindy's voice, loud and angry, rang through the barn. Christina glanced around to see whom Cindy was yelling at, but there was no one in sight, only the black mare.

"Who said you have to be a groom?" Christina asked, staring at Cindy.

"Your mom seems to think I need to keep myself occupied," Cindy replied. "I told her I'd be glad to help out, but this wasn't what I had in mind."

Christina frowned. "If you can't ride, at least you can handle the horses," she offered. "It won't be long until you can ride again."

Cindy glared at her. "I should be riding right now," she said. She grabbed Sassy's lead line and opened the stall door. "Move over," she said in a harsh voice. Sassy flicked her ears at Cindy's tone, then shifted to the side. Cindy quickly clipped the lead to the mare's halter. "Let's go," she said to the mare, giving a firm pull on the lead line. Sassy stiffened, raising her head. "What's this nonsense?" Cindy demanded, her tone sharp.

Christina frowned. "Sassy likes to have her whorl rubbed," she offered. "Then she'll follow you any-where."

Cindy tilted her head and sighed. "She needs to fol-low me because I say so, Christina. Not because I sweet-talk her into it."

"Okay," Christina said as Cindy led Sassy out of the barn. "But if you don't want to groom, maybe you should talk to my mom about it. There's lots of other stuff to do around here." It was probably a good thing Cindy didn't want to be around the horses. She didn't seem to have much sensitivity toward them.

She rode Mischief Maker onto the track, still per-turbed by Cindy's bad mood, and even more dis-tressed over Star. She wanted to talk to Melanie, but her cousin was on Raven, and the high-strung filly kept her full attention.

As she circled the track, Christina saw Cindy lead Sassy Jazz down the tractor lane between the pad-docks. Cindy paused to watch Melanie and Raven whiz by at a full gallop. Cindy's shoulders sagged, and she turned away, trudging along the fence line once more. Christina felt bad to see Cindy so depressed. Maybe she just needed to be more understanding of Cindy's situation.

But when Christina was leaving the barn after putting her tack away, she passed Cindy sitting outside on a hay bale, cleaning tack. Christina's sympathetic words died on her lips at the sight of the surly expression on Cindy's face, and she hurried by without a word. Injury or no injury, whether she could ride or not, Cindy had a bad attitude.

"Are you sure you don't want to go shopping with Katie and me?" Melanie asked as they walked out of their driver education class that afternoon. "After we're done looking for clothes, we could try that new Thai take-out place in Lexington," she added temptingly.

Christina shook her head firmly. "I want to be home in case there's any word on Star," she said. "But you guys have fun."

"We will," Melanie said. Then her smile faded to concern. "I hope Star's okay," she added.

"Me too," Christina said, shoving her books in her locker and hurriedly slamming it shut.

When she reached the bus stop, she paused on the sidewalk to scan the parking lot hopefully.

"Hey, Chris! Over here!"

To her delight, she saw Parker Townsend standing near his pickup. He waved to her, and she hurried across the lot.

Dressed in a polo shirt and tan breeches, Parker looked like the professional horseman he was. He and his bay mare, Foxy, were hoping to be selected for the Olympics in three-day eventing.

"I'm so glad to see you," Christina said, rising onto her tiptoes to touch her lips to his. "When you didn't call back on Sunday night, I thought maybe you'd forgotten all about me."

Parker smiled down at her. "Not a chance," he said. "I didn't even get the message until today. The new housekeeper keeps forgetting to write things down," he explained. "Mom has missed a couple of her big social gatherings because of it. And we all know that no one messes with Lavinia Townsend's social life."

Christina would have laughed, but Parker's words were too close to the truth. She wouldn't be at all surprised if the housekeeper was fired within the week.

"Anyway, I thought maybe you'd decided to stay in New York with Star," Parker went on, "but then I heard Dad telling Dunkirk he talked to you and your mom yesterday." He pulled the passenger door open for her.

"You heard about that, huh?" Christina said as she

slid into the pickup. Parker gave her a sympathetic look.

"I'm on my way to Whisperwood to teach a couple of classes for Sam," Parker said. "I figured you'd need a lift home."

"I do," Christina said. "And I'm glad to see you, too."

Parker flashed her a smile. "Me too," he said. "It'll be nice when Star's back from New York and you aren't gone every weekend. Maybe then we can act like normal people and see a movie or go out to dinner or something."

"That would be different, wouldn't it?" Christina agreed. "I feel like I've barely been home at all. But in a couple more weeks the Champagne will be over, and we're bringing Star home to start conditioning him for the Derby prep races. Then we can see each other more, I promise."

Parker turned onto Whitebrook's long gravel drive.

"You can just drop me here," Christina said as Parker pulled up near the main stable. "Thanks so much for coming to get me."

"I'll be at Whisperwood for a couple of hours if you want to come over and watch me teach the kids," Parker said, leaning over to kiss Christina on the cheek.

"I'd love to," she said. "I'll see you later." She

climbed from the truck and hurried into the barn, going straight to her mother's office. As she made her way down the barn aisle Christina realized she hadn't told Parker how worried she was about Star. They had always shared everything; there just hadn't been time. She would have to tell him all about it as soon as she got a chance. Parker always knew how to cheer her up.

Ashleigh was seated at her desk, examining some papers.

"Have you heard anything?" Christina asked, sitting on the chair near the door. "Is Star any better?"

Ashleigh started to shake her head when the phone rang. Christina rose to leave as Ashleigh cradled the receiver on her shoulder.

"Hi, Maureen," she said, gesturing for Christina to stay. "What's up?"

Christina sat down again, staring across the desk at Ashleigh. There was a moment of silence while the assistant trainer spoke. Ashleigh's eyes widened and she sat up straight, gripping the receiver tightly. Christina watched anxiously, wishing she could hear what Maureen was saying.

"But the vets don't know what it is?" Ashleigh asked, sounding worried.

Christina wanted to grab the phone, but she clenched her hands in her lap, her body rigid as she waited for the call to end.

"Okay," Ashleigh finally said. "Bringing him home is the best idea. Thank Vince for offering to send him down in his van. I appreciate it." Ashleigh hung up and sighed heavily, rubbing her fingertips across her forehead.

"What?" Christina demanded. "What's wrong with Star?"

Ashleigh looked up, a grim expression on her face. "He won't eat," she said. "He's lethargic, and he's starting to show the same symptoms as Fire 'n' Ice. Vince is having him shipped home. They're leaving right away, so they should be here late tomorrow."

Christina pressed her knuckles to her mouth, her mind reeling. "What is it?" she asked. "What does he have?"

Ashleigh clasped her hands together, resting them on the desk. She shook her head slowly. "The vets can't identify anything," she said. "There is some concern that the other colt was exposed to a tropical virus while he was at Gulfstream Park, but until they do more testing and check with the Florida track, they can't tell us anything."

Christina rose woodenly and turned to leave the office. She never should have left Star at Belmont. She had known something was wrong, but she'd ignored what her heart was telling her. She should have made her parents listen to her. If Star was seriously ill, she would hold herself responsible. How could she have left him at Belmont when he was suffering?

She trudged up the barn aisle and walked to the house slowly, burdened with worry about her colt. She called Whisperwood, leaving a message to let Parker know she wouldn't be coming over, and she did her homework without even thinking about what she was studying. Although she ate the food her father made for dinner, she didn't taste any of it. Mike and Ashleigh were quiet throughout the meal, and as soon as it was over, Christina went to her room, her thoughts focused on Star and how she had left him in New York, sick. She had let him down.

She heard Katie's car pull up in front of the house and Melanie's voice drift up from the living room when she came into the house, but she didn't go downstairs to see her. Instead, she got ready for bed, staring at herself in the mirror as she brushed her teeth. She had failed Star when he needed her most. How could she forgive herself?

When she returned to her room, Melanie was sitting on her bed.

"Is there anything I can do?" her cousin asked worriedly.

Christina shook her head. "Thanks, Mel. Mom says we just have to wait until Star gets home and take it from there. He'll be here tomorrow, after school."

The next day passed in a nightmarish blur. Christina had always been a good student, but she had trouble focusing in her classes. At lunchtime she dug change from her pocket and used the pay phone in the school to call the barn office at Whitebrook. Ian answered.

"They'll be here right after you get home from school, Chris," he said. "We have everything set up, and your mom put a call in to Dr. Lanum. We're doing everything we can."

"I know," she said. "Thank you, Ian."

Christina hurried to her next class, and the next, sitting quietly until the bell rang, not hearing a word the teachers said. Finally the day ended and she hurried out to the bus. Melanie was staying after school to retake a geometry test she'd had trouble with, so Christina sat alone on the bus, staring blindly out the window.

Heavy clouds were starting to fill the sky, adding to Christina's bleak mood. The trip home seemed to take an eternity, but finally the driver pulled to a stop at the end of Whitebrook's long driveway.

Since there was no sign of any activity at the barn, Christina went to the house first. She changed quickly, then hurried back to the stables so that she could be there when Star got home. The rain started to fall before she reached the barn, heavy drops that pelted the ground angrily. Christina barely noticed that her thin jacket was already soaked through by the time she got inside.

Ian was in the office, on the phone. When he hung up he was frowning. "Dr. Lanum is running late," he said, drumming his fingers on the desk. "The office is having trouble tracking her down." He eyed Christina up and down, then pointed at a row of hooks on the wall, where some old barn jackets were hanging. "Change that coat," he said. "There's no sense in your catching a cold." He popped a Whitebrook baseball cap on her head.

"Thanks, Ian," she said quietly, wrapping the warm coat around herself.

The rumbling sound of a horse van coming up the driveway drew Christina and Ian from the office. They met Mike and Ashleigh outside the barn and watched Vince's van pull to a stop. Mike draped his arm over Christina's shoulder, giving her a comforting squeeze.

"We'll get him through this in no time," he said confidently.

Christina wondered if her father was as sure as he sounded. She hurried to the back of the van as Vince's driver opened the tailgate, and peered inside.

Star stood in the dark interior, his head low and his ears limp. Christina's heart plummeted and her breath caught in her throat to see her colt looking so wretched.

"Star," she said softly, "you're home, boy. I'm here with you."

Star raised his head, flicking his ears and turning toward her. Christina reached in to catch his lead and gave it a gentle tug. When he came out of the van, the colt's steps were sluggish. He stopped just outside the van and rested his chin on Christina's shoulder, sighing deeply as if he'd suffered through a terrible ordeal. Christina choked down a sob.

The wet, gloomy weather only made things seem that much worse.

She reached up to wipe away the drops of rain that had fallen on the colt. "We'll take care of you, boy. Everything is all right now."

"Let's get him in his stall," Ashleigh said, worry lines creasing her forehead.

Christina led the despondent colt toward his usual stall, eager to be alone with him.

"No, Chris." Ashleigh stopped her. "We set up an isolation stall for him. We can't risk having him around the other horses."

Christina felt her heart wrench, but she followed her mother, who led the way to a stall at the far end of the barn.

"I'm sorry, boy," Christina told Star. "I should have

known you didn't feel well. You tried to tell me Sunday, didn't you? This is my fault. If we'd brought you home sooner, you wouldn't have gotten sick. I just know it."

"This isn't your fault," Ashleigh said, opening the stall door. Christina led Star inside. The deep bedding rustled under their feet. She unbuckled Star's halter and smoothed his mane into place. "As soon as Star came into contact with Fire'n'Ice, he probably caught whatever it is. Even the people working with Fire'n'Ice didn't know he was sick. There was no way to have known. Remember that, Chris. There's nothing you could have done."

Christina didn't answer. She stood silently by Star's side, stroking his soft neck over and over as he sniffed the fresh bedding on the floor of his stall.

"I'm going to call Brad," Ashleigh said, and turned to go.

Christina wanted to protest. She was sure Brad would try to blame Star's illness on her, but she knew he was interested in the colt's well-being, too—even if it was for reasons different from her own. She waited for her mother to return, still softly stroking the chestnut colt.

"Brad is sending his vet over," Ashleigh announced when she came back.

"What about our regular vets?" Christina asked. "If

you can't reach Dr. Lanum, what about Dr. Seymour?"

"Neither of them is available," Ashleigh said. "We need someone now, Chris. Brad has as much a right to choose a vet as we do. He uses only the best vets for his horses, so don't worry."

"He doesn't look that bad, Mom," Christina said urgently. "He'll be fine in time to go back to Belmont and run in the Champagne, won't he?"

At the look on Ashleigh's face, Christina's breath stuck in her throat. She struggled to inhale. "What?" she demanded. "What aren't you telling me? What does he have?"

Ashleigh shook her head. "No one knows, Christina. I called Belmont again. The other horse is showing signs of paralysis now. The vets don't know what's causing it. We have to remain optimistic, but until we know what's going on, we can't make any plans for the future."

Ashleigh squeezed her hand and then left her alone with Star. Christina sank down in the thick bedding, looking up at the listless colt.

"You have to be all right," she said. Star gazed down at her through heavy-lidded eyes, and Christina fought back her tears. She wished she were in the middle of a nightmare, but she knew she was wide awake.

7

WHEN CHRISTINA HEARD FOOTSTEPS AND A STRANGE VOICE in the aisle, she scrambled to her feet and stood between Star and the door. If the new veterinarian acted anything like Brad or Ralph Dunkirk, she wasn't going to let him touch Star.

Coming toward them were Ian, Brad, and a tall, thin man carrying a medical bag. The vet was wearing worn coveralls and had a kindly, worried expression.

When they reached Star's stall, Brad looked past Christina and scowled at Star, then shook his head in disgust. "He'd better pull through this," he said to Ian. "I'm holding Whitebrook responsible if we lose him."

Ian ignored the comment, but Christina bristled.

Before she could say anything, the vet silenced Brad. "Let me take a look at him," the vet said calmly.

92

"It would be helpful to know what we're dealing with."

He turned to the stall and smiled at Christina. "Hi there," he said, extending his hand. "I'm Dr. Stevens. I take it this is the patient?"

Christina felt her defensiveness slip away at the veterinarian's friendly demeanor. "This is Star," she said, moving out of the way so that the vet could see the colt. Star's head seemed too heavy for his neck. He stood quietly, his eyes half closed and his legs splayed. When Dr. Stevens entered the stall, the lethargic colt barely moved his head.

Even though it didn't seem necessary, she held Star's head while Dr. Stevens started his examination. Star rested his nose in the crook of Christina's elbow, leaning heavily against her side. Christina blinked back tears while she stroked his neck.

Brad stood in the aisle with Ian, looking grim. "That colt is far too valuable to lose to some random virus," he said irritably.

Christina tightened her grip on Star's halter and tensed her jaw to keep from snapping at Brad. Dr. Stevens glanced at her, then gave a tiny wink and shook his head slightly. Christina decided she liked Dr. Stevens, even if he did work for Brad.

"Let's go down to the office," Ian said to Brad, herding him away from the stall. "Ashleigh is on the phone to New York again, trying to get more information on the other colt that took sick."

"Thank you, Ian," Christina muttered under her breath as the two men walked away.

Dr. Stevens shot her an amused look before he continued his examination. "Sorry about that," he said, running his hands along Star's top line. "Brad can be a little blunt when he's worried."

Christina curled her lip. All Brad was worried about was losing money. He didn't care one bit about Star. "Star is special," she said. "He isn't just a racehorse. Not to me, anyway," she amended.

"I can tell," the vet said, cocking his head as he listened to Star's heartbeat. Finally Dr. Stevens stepped back, a puzzled look on his face. "We'll draw some blood," he said. "I know they ran some tests up at Belmont, but we'll do a more comprehensive screening and see if there's something we can identify so we can focus our treatment."

Ashleigh came down the aisle, the cordless phone in her hand, with Ian and Brad right behind her. "It's the vet at Belmont," she said, holding the phone out to Dr. Stevens. "He wants to talk to you."

The lost look on Ashleigh's face filled Christina with fear. She watched anxiously while Dr. Stevens listened to the vet on the other end of the line, a deep frown furrowing his brow. She wrapped her arms protectively around Star's head, and the colt leaned his nose against her, sighing deeply.

Finally the vet ended the call. He looked at Brad and Ashleigh, then at Star and Christina. "The other colt is down," he said. "They don't hold out much hope for him."

Christina inhaled sharply and hugged Star's head close. "Star is going to be okay," she said. "He has to be."

The vet studied Star. "Right now Star seems to be exhibiting the same symptoms the other colt did in the early stages. Luckily there are no signs of paralysis. Since none of the drugs they've tried on the horse at Belmont have helped, all we can do is keep watching."

Christina felt her legs go weak. She braced herself against the side of the stall, still cradling Star's head. "We'll try everything we possibly can from the medical side of things," Dr. Stevens promised her. "But he's going to need a lot of attention."

"And he'll get it," Christina said firmly, standing straight. "Just tell me what I need to do." She rested her hand on the colt's neck and looked evenly at the vet.

"I'll leave a list of instructions in the office," Dr. Stevens said.

"Don't you think he should be at your clinic?" Brad asked, sounding skeptical. "So you can keep an eye on him?"

Christina stiffened, but Dr. Stevens was already shaking his head. "I think Star is in the best place he can be," he said to Brad. "The colt is in good hands right here."

Brad scowled, but Christina felt a rush of gratitude toward Dr. Stevens. "I won't leave him for a minute," she promised.

"I'll be by daily to check on him," the vet said. "But if he shows any new symptoms, I want to be notified immediately."

"I'll be checking on Star regularly, too," Brad added, eyeing the listless colt. "He'd better pull through this. Losing him would be a big setback for Townsend Acres."

Christina was about to say something to Brad, but she caught herself and looked at Dr. Stevens instead. "Thank you," she said to the vet, hating the helpless feeling that shrouded her. She stroked Star's neck, watching the vet head for the office with Ian and Brad.

Ashleigh hesitated by the stall, her expression one of grim determination. "We'll get him through this, Chris," she said. "He's a fighter. He'll pull through."

"I know," Christina said, massaging the base of Star's ear. "And I'm not leaving him alone until he's better."

"I need to get down to the office so I can get Dr. Stevens's instructions firsthand. Are you okay?"

Christina nodded silently. Ashleigh left, and Christina gazed at Star, who dropped his head even lower, his eyes almost shut. "You have to get better, Star. Do you understand? Whatever is wrong, you have to get over it. I'll do everything I can to help you, okay?"

She refilled Star's water bucket and headed for the storage room to get him a blanket. When she returned, Dani was outside Star's stall. "I'll fix up a nice mash for him," the groom said. "I'm so sorry, Chris."

"It isn't your fault," Christina said. "It's no one's fault." *Except mine,* she berated herself silently.

"I'm sure he'll get better fast now that he's home," Dani said, then headed for the feed room, leaving Christina alone with Star.

"You *are* going to get better, right, boy?" she asked, rubbing his neck. Star sighed and leaned into her, as though he barely had the strength to stay standing.

Christina held the pan while Star halfheartedly tasted the mix of bran, oats, molasses, and grated apples Dani had prepared.

"Come on, boy," Christina pleaded. "Just a few bites?" Star nosed through the pan, lipping at the mash, chewing languidly on a few grains. Finally he turned away from the food. Christina sighed and took the pan out of his stall. "We're going to do everything Dr. Stevens said," she told the colt. "You're going to get over this."

Star lifted his head slightly and looked at her.

"You have a lot of races to run, Star," she said. "You're going to be fine."

Christina stayed at Star's side late into the night, reluctant to leave him. When her feet grew tired from standing, she sat in the corner of the stall, talking to the colt all the while.

"You need to get a good night's sleep," Ashleigh said, ordering Christina to the house. "You won't be any help to him if you let yourself get run down."

Christina went to bed but stayed wide awake, staring up at the dark ceiling. There was no way she could fall asleep knowing Star was down in the barn all alone, feeling sick. She got up and dragged on her jeans and a sweatshirt, making as little noise as possible on her way downstairs. She pulled on a pair of boots and a jacket and hurried out to the barn once more.

Star grunted softly when she reached his stall. Christina spread a wool horse blanket on the floor of the stall and lay down on it. Star ambled over to her and rested his chin on her shoulder, breathing softly into her hair. Finally Christina fell asleep with her hand on his nose.

"I figured I'd find you here."

At the sound of Melanie's voice, Christina snapped

awake. She looked around, feeling a little disoriented, but then she remembered why she was sleeping in Star's stall. The colt was still standing over her, bleary-eyed and listless.

"You'd better get up to the house and change before your mom sees you," Melanie said. "I told her I'd get you up this morning. She thinks you're still in bed."

Christina rose slowly and stretched her stiff muscles. Star gazed at her through heavy-lidded eyes, and she stroked his white star gently. "I couldn't leave him down here alone," she said. "He needs me."

"I know," Melanie said, tucking her blond hair behind her ears. "I'll cover for you until you get back."

"Thanks, Mel," Christina said. She hurried up to the house and washed her face. Then she changed her clothes and returned to the barn.

"You'd better clean Star's stall and disinfect his supplies this morning," Ashleigh said. "I've asked Naomi to ride your assigned horses."

Christina nodded and reached for a pitchfork, grateful that her mother hadn't noticed she'd spent the night in the barn.

She stripped Star's stall, working around the spirit-less colt and stopping frequently to stroke his nose. "You're going to be fine, Star," she kept telling him, wishing he looked less lethargic. When she was done with her chores, she set up a folding chair in front of the stall and sat down to keep vigil.

"Chris, you still have to go to school," Ashleigh said as she came out of the barn office.

"But Mom," Christina started to protest.

Ashleigh shook her head firmly. "No buts," she said. "Dr. Stevens will be by in a couple of hours. You go get ready for school. I'll watch him for you, I promise."

Reluctantly Christina left Star's side to change her clothes. When she ran down the driveway, the bus was just pulling in.

School passed in a blur. The teachers seemed to be talking in slow motion, and Christina's feet felt heavy as she made her way from class to class. At last the final bell rang, and she flew outside and onto the bus. When she got home, there was a message from Vince Jones in the barn office. "He wants to know if you're going up to Belmont this weekend to work Gratis," Ashleigh said, handing her the paper with Vince's number at the Belmont track. "You're still down to race him in the Futurity, remember."

"I can't," Christina exclaimed. "I'm not leaving Star. No way."

Ashleigh nodded. "I understand, but I told him you would call."

Christina dialed the number to Vince's office at the track and got his voice mail. She left a message telling him she'd keep him posted on Star's condition but that she couldn't promise she'd be able to race Gratis in the Futurity, and she definitely wouldn't be flying to New York to work him that weekend.

"I can't believe you did that," Cindy said from the office doorway.

"Did what?" Christina asked, surprised at the disgusted tone in Cindy's voice.

"You just told a top trainer you couldn't ride his horse in an important race," Cindy said, shaking her head. "You must have more rides than you know what to do with."

Christina looked down at her hands. "Star is sick," she said quietly. "Until I know what's wrong with him and he starts getting better, I'm not leaving him."

Cindy snorted in disbelief. "Vince can replace you in a heartbeat, you know. Do you realize how many jockeys want to ride for him?"

Christina swallowed hard. She did know. She'd worked hard to get Vince to allow her to ride for him, and she'd struggled with Gratis to prove to Vince she deserved the chance to ride him. And now she might be throwing it away, but Star was more important than her racing career. He was more important than anything else in her life.

"Vince can get another jockey. I don't care. I can't desert Star. He needs me."

"Do you know how long it took me to get rides from top trainers like Vince?" Cindy demanded. "You just don't appreciate all the opportunities you're being given."

"I wasn't given anything," Christina exclaimed. "I earned the chance to ride for Vince."

"Whatever. You're throwing your whole career away," Cindy muttered, and walked off.

Christina watched her go, her heart pounding. Maybe she *was* blowing her future by turning Vince down, but her mind wouldn't be on her riding anyway, not until Star was all right. Nothing else mattered; she had to stay with Star.

Christina hurried down to the isolation stall, where her mother was sitting in the aisle, looking over some printed pages. Behind her, Star lifted his head and nickered softly at Christina. Delighted to see him show a little spirit, she slipped into the stall and stroked his nose. "What did Dr. Stevens say?" Christina asked her mother.

"Still no concrete information," Ashleigh said distractedly. "He brought these articles from veterinary journals. He thought we might notice some similarities and things to watch for. He'll call back later."

"Is Star eating and drinking?" Christina asked. "He

hardly ate any of his dinner last night."

Ashleigh held up the clipboard with Dr. Stevens's instructions, and a chart that listed how much Star had eaten and how much medicine he'd been given.

"He did eat," Christina said excitedly. "That's great!"

Ashleigh nodded. "I had Cindy walk him up and down the aisle for a while to keep him from getting stiff standing around in his stall. I hope he'll snap out of this quickly. But right now you have chores to do."

"Why Cindy?" Christina asked. She didn't like the idea of Cindy handling Star. Cindy was too impatient. "Why can't Dani take care of him?"

"Dani has a lot of other work to do," her mother said. "Cindy is free during the day. I've asked her to keep a close eye on Star."

Christina pinched her mouth shut. She couldn't say anything to her mother about Cindy, but she hated the thought of Cindy talking to Star the way she did to the other horses, particularly when he was so sick and needed especially gentle care.

After doing her barn chores, Christina returned to Star's stall. "I'm back, boy," she sang out, stepping inside. But the colt didn't even look up, and Christina felt her heart clench. She began to massage his back, working from his poll to his tail, the way Ian had taught her long ago. According to Dr. Stevens's instructions, keeping Star's circulation going was very important.

"I could use a back rub, too," Parker said from outside the stall.

"Parker!" Christina cried. In spite of the worry she felt for Star, her heart gave a happy little skip at the sight of her boyfriend's face.

"I went by school to give you a ride home, but you were already gone. I brought Mel home instead. She told me all about Star. How's he doing?" Parker asked, leaning against the stall door.

"He ate a little," Christina answered, trying to sound optimistic. She stroked the colt's neck, tears misting her eyes. "He's going to be fine, aren't you, Star?"

Star sighed and dropped his head, closing his eyes.

Parker reached out and smoothed back Christina's hair. "It's good that he ate," he said encouragingly.

Christina came out of the stall, and Parker slipped his arm around her waist. "Let's take a little walk," he said. "You look like you could use a break."

Christina glanced at Star. The colt was standing quietly. He looked more tired than sick. But Fire 'n' Ice hadn't looked sick, either, and now he was suffering from paralysis. At least Star was still walking and eating—that was a good sign.

"A walk sounds good," Christina said. "I need to wash my hands first, though. They still don't know what caused Star to get sick. I don't want to spread whatever it is anywhere else on the farm."

While Parker waited, Christina scrubbed with hot water and soap all the way up to her elbows, the way Dr. Stevens had told them all to do. Then she took Parker's hand, and they strolled out of the barn and up to the grass pastures behind the house. The weanlings were out grazing, and Christina opened the gate so that she and Parker could go into the field.

Curious, the young horses began to follow them. Christina and Parker stopped, letting the colts and fillies mill around them, snorting and sniffing their clothes with interest. Christina loved the leggy, spirited weanlings. She remembered how feisty and rambunctious Star had been at their age. He was only two, but he was so different now.

"Your dad was really upset about Star," Christina said, holding her hand out so that Silver Jane's bay filly, Pride's Best, could sniff her fingertips.

Parker winced, running his hand along another filly's shoulder. The weanling looked just like her mother, Perfect Heart, from her rich chestnut coat to the heart-shaped star on her forehead. "You know Dad," he said. "Don't let him get to you, Chris."

"I try not to," Christina replied, pushing Miss America's bold black colt away as he tasted the leg of her jeans with his little teeth. There was a slight commotion as the weanlings jostled each other. Pride's Best squealed, then spun around and took off at a gallop across the paddock. The rest of the young horses followed, leaving Christina and Parker alone in the middle of the field.

Christina watched the running foals for a moment before Parker took her hand and they walked back to the gate.

Christina squeezed Parker's hand tightly. "I wish your dad didn't get to you, either."

"I'm used to it." Parker shrugged as he unlatched the gate. "Look, Chris, I'd love to stay and watch Star with you, but I need to get over to Whisperwood," he said. "Sam and Tor are going out to dinner, so I said I'd feed the horses for them."

"That's all right," Christina said, walking Parker to his truck. "I'm glad you came by."

"Don't worry, Chris. Star's going to be all right," Parker said, hugging her before he drove off. Christina watched him go, then returned to the barn. Star hadn't moved. He barely blinked when she opened his stall door. Christina wrapped her arms around his neck, and Star sighed, as if just breathing was a major effort.

"I'm so sorry you're sick, Star," she murmured, fighting down the bleak sense of helplessness that threatened to overwhelm her. She stayed beside him, stroking his neck and talking to him softly. "I wish I knew what to do to make you better."

Without being able to identify the disease, the veterinarian wouldn't know how to treat it. That meant that if Star was going to overcome his illness, he had to do it on his own. "I'll be here with you, Star," Christina promised. "Whatever made you sick, we'll fight it together."

8

"HEY, CHRIS!"

At the sound of Katie Garrity's voice, Christina turned away from the crowd of students waiting at the bus stop. Katie, Chad Walker, Kaitlin Boyce, and a couple of other seniors were walking along the sidewalk in front of the school. It was Thursday afternoon, the day had been impossibly long, and the only thing on Christina's mind was getting home to Star.

But they stopped near her, and Christina smiled at the cheerful-looking group. "How's Sterling?" she asked Kaitlin, who was leasing the mare from Sam and Tor.

"She's great," Kaitlin said happily. "I just love jumping her. We're having so much fun."

Christina smiled, but she couldn't think of anything to say in response. She was sincerely pleased that her eventing mare was being so well cared for and loved, but her happiness for Kaitlin was clouded by thoughts of Star. Everything beyond Star's immediate needs seemed to be happening on another planet, a million miles away.

"We're the planning committee for Spirit Week this year," Katie said. "We could use another person if you want to join, Chris. We're having our first meeting this afternoon."

"Spirit Week?" Christina echoed blankly. She had completely forgotten about the school's fall activities.

Katie laughed. "Hello? Chris? We had a senior class meeting this morning to discuss it. The homecoming game is in six weeks, and we're going to make this year's Spirit Week the best ever." Katie paused and frowned at Christina. "Are you okay?"

"I'm fine," Christina said, blushing. She glanced at her bus stop, but the bus still hadn't arrived. She didn't want to have to explain about Star to all these people. All she wanted to do was go home and see the colt. Spirit Week just didn't seem very important when Star was sick.

"You're a jockey, aren't you?" a blond girl standing near Chad asked. "I saw you on television. My dad watches all the races." She stared wide-eyed at Christina. "I can't imagine riding that fast."

"Yeah," Katie said with a grin. "I always thought you'd end up on the United States equestrian team, Chris. But it looks like you're addicted to racing now."

Christina smiled politely. If Star didn't recover from his illness, she didn't know if she'd ever want to race again. Her bus finally pulled into the lot. "There's my ride," she said. "I need to get home. I'll see you all later."

She hefted her book bag onto her shoulder and headed for the school bus, wishing Melanie were with her. But Melanie had gone to Fredericka's farm to talk to her about Image. Christina was glad that Melanie had found Image, a horse she felt as passionate about as Christina did about Star. But right now she needed to talk to someone who could understand how hard it was to see Star suffer.

When the bus finally dropped her off at Whitebrook, Christina hurried up the tree-lined drive and went straight to the barn. Ashleigh was standing at Star's stall, a thermometer in her hand. She glanced up, shaking her head when she saw Christina.

Christina felt her heart sink at the bleak expression on her mother's face. "What is it?" she asked, dropping her bag outside the stall. Star's only reaction to Christina's arrival was to twitch his nostrils.

"He's got a fever," Ashleigh said. "I've called Dr. Stevens. He'll be here right away." The ringing of the phone drew Ashleigh away. "That may be the clinic," she said, striding toward the office.

Christina went into his stall, and Star raised his head a fraction of an inch, nickering weakly to her. She pulled the colt's blanket off and began to groom him. She couldn't tell if he was enjoying it or not, but it seemed important that he know she was there for him.

While Christina waited with Star for the vet to arrive, Jonnie and Joe came by the stall. Joe held out a bright red apple. "This is for Star when he gets to feeling better," the groom said, handing it to Christina. "If there's anything we can do, Chris, you just speak up, okay?"

"Thanks, Joe," Christina said, grateful for their support.

Jonnie nodded confidently. "Star's going to get better, Chris. I know he will."

When the grooms went back to work, she turned to Star. "Everyone is pulling for you, Star. You've got to get better, okay?"

When Dr. Stevens arrived, he checked Star over thoroughly, shaking his head in confusion. "This is such a mystery," he said, frowning deeply. "There isn't a test we haven't done to try to identify the cause of this. I wish I could give you a clear answer," he said to Ashleigh and Christina. "But right now all we can do is keep treating the symptoms."

Dr. Stevens left more medications and gave Star penicillin and some vitamin boosters. "He's still drinking, and he's eating a little," he said. "That's a good sign. His system hasn't shut down."

When he left, Christina stayed by Star's side, stroking his shoulder. "I don't know what I'd do if anything happened to you, Star," she murmured. "You need to start getting better."

Cindy came by the stall with a fresh pan of mash. "Your mom said to try to get him to eat some of this," she said, handing the pan to Christina.

While Star nosed through the food, Cindy sat down on the chair in front of his stall, then jumped up and paced a few steps.

"What's wrong?" Christina asked, holding the pan steady as Star took a bite. She was heartened to see him showing some appetite, even if it was just for a few bites of food.

"Sitting around here is making me crazy," Cindy exclaimed, wrinkling up her face. "I'm used to being constantly on the go." She paced a few more steps, reminding Christina of a caged tiger. "If I can't start riding, I'm going to miss out on the rest of the Belmont meet. I won't be in good enough shape to race anywhere if I can't even work out."

"You must miss all your friends in New York, too," Christina observed.

Cindy stopped pacing and stared at Christina for a long time before she spoke. "I've never had time for friends," she said. "I've put all my energy into racing. Everyone I know competes with me for rides and wins." She laughed harshly. "And look where it's gotten me," she said.

Christina gaped at her. No wonder Cindy didn't know how to have a friendly conversation. She'd never had any friends!

Star lost interest in the grain, and he turned away.

"I'll take that," Cindy offered.

Christina handed her the grain pan and left Star alone for a few minutes while she walked outside. She stopped in the middle of the big yard and looked around at the sprawling buildings that made up Whitebrook. The next week flatbed trucks would bring the materials to build the walls and roof of the addition to the stallion barn. In the white-fenced paddocks, graceful Thoroughbreds grazed, and overhead, puffy clouds floated in the clear blue sky.

Christina tried to imagine living alone in a New York apartment, not being able to walk down to the barn or go for a hack over the wooded trails surrounding Whitebrook.

Raised voices behind her drew her attention back to the barn. Cindy and Ian were standing just inside the barn, facing each other.

113

"You have to let me start working some horses," she heard Cindy say. "I've never gone this many days without riding."

"I can't let you, Cindy," Ian responded, crossing his arms in front of his chest. "Doctor's orders."

"It won't hurt anything to let me exercise-ride some of the three-year-olds." Cindy argued.

"I want to see something from your doctor first," Ian said. "I don't want you injuring yourself even worse. Then you may never, ever ride again—is that what you want?"

"I just need to rebuild the muscles in my shoulder," Cindy insisted.

But Ian shook his head firmly. "If it's okay with Ashleigh and Mike, you could help with the ground work," he said. "I know it isn't the same thing as being on horseback, but it's the best I can offer you."

Christina headed for the house. She didn't want Ian and Cindy to know she'd been listening in on their private conversation.

She called Parker, but he was out. Then she dug through the refrigerator and returned to the barn with a handful of baby carrots, determined to tempt Star into eating more.

By the time she returned to the barn, Ian was in the weanling pasture with Maureen, looking over the foals that gamboled around the field. An unbidden smile twitched at Christina's mouth. The lively foals frolicked and raced because it felt good. She remembered how when Star was just a foal, his head would spring up, his ears would prick forward, and, as if a starting bell had gone off in his head, the colt would break into a dead run and gallop around the paddock, just for the joy of running.

She hurried back to Star's stall, her happy thoughts fading when she saw how downtrodden the colt looked right then.

"You can't let this beat you," she said, entering the stall. "You've got to try, Star. Try as hard as you can."

Star turned his nose away from the carrot bits Christina offered him, so she knelt down and massaged his legs, trying to work some life into them. Then she slipped his halter on and led him from his stall, walking him up and down the unoccupied end of the barn. Star plodded after her, barely lifting his hooves from the ground. After they had paced the aisle a few times, Christina returned the colt to his stall.

Star lowered his head and groaned softly, then released a deep sigh and closed his eyes, standing quietly while Christina finished rubbing him down. She'd never seen him so lackluster. Even his eyes seemed glazed.

"My turn to stand watch," Dani said, walking up to the stall. "Your mom says you're supposed to get up to the house and get ready for dinner."

Christina didn't feel like eating and socializing, but Beth had invited them to the cottage for dinner to celebrate Cindy's homecoming, and Christina knew her parents would be upset if she didn't go.

"I'll be back soon," she promised Star, then headed for the house to shower and change. An hour later Christina and Melanie walked over to the McLeans' cottage with Mike and Ashleigh.

Kevin answered the door, a cordless phone in one hand. "Sam and Tor are in the dining room with Dad," he said, gesturing toward the middle of the house.

He held the phone back up to his ear. "Sorry, Lindsey," he said into the receiver. Christina shot a quick look at Melanie. To Christina's relief, her cousin looked unperturbed by the phone conversation. Obviously Melanie was past being jealous of Kevin's new girlfriend.

Ashleigh led the way to the dining room, where Samantha was setting the table. Ian's elder daughter had her red hair hanging loose, flowing in a wavy curtain down her back.

Ian came out of the kitchen, a huge bowl of salad in his hands, with Sam's husband, Tor, right behind him, carrying a basket of his famous homemade rolls.

"I forgot how good Beth's cooking is," Cindy said,

walking in with a soup tureen. "I have to be careful. If I stay here long, I'll put on a ton of weight."

"How's your shoulder?" Mike asked, taking the tureen from her and setting it on the table.

"I saw the doctor today," Cindy said. "It won't be long before I'm riding again."

But when they sat down to eat, Christina noticed that Cindy was resting her left hand in her lap, keeping her shoulder still. No one else seemed to notice, and the meal passed in a flurry of conversation about Sam and Tor's work at Whisperwood, remodeling the stallion barn, and Melanie and Image. Cindy didn't talk much, and Christina barely spoke or ate. No one said a word about the fact that Cindy might never race again, or that Star was sick, maybe even dying. It was all Christina could do to sit through dinner before she raced back to the barn to check on Star.

Saturday morning Christina was in Star's stall, grooming the colt and trying to tempt him to eat, when Brad came by. He stood in front of Star's stall, shaking his head disgustedly. "He's never going to be back on top for the Derby," Brad said.

"I don't care," Christina said, surprising herself when she realized she really *didn't* care about the Derby. All she cared about was Star getting better. She

117

draped her arm around the colt's neck and gave Brad a defiant look. "If you don't want him anymore," she added, "I'll still buy him from you."

Brad gave her a sour look and walked away without another word.

"Let's get you out of here and walk a little bit," she said to Star, clipping the lead line onto his halter. She walked slowly down the unoccupied end of the barn, keeping Star well away from the other horses. With every shuffling step he took, her heart sank lower. "You're not going to give up, Star," she said desperately. "Do you hear me?"

Star heaved a deep sigh, and Christina walked him back to his stall, her lower lip quivering as she fought back her tears.

Parker called to check on Star's condition, and Mike handed her the cordless phone. All Christina could tell him was that nothing had changed.

"That could be good," Parker said encouragingly. "He's still walking, right? And eating?"

"Yes," Christina replied. She sat down near Star's stall, the cordless phone cradled between her ear and her shoulder. "But no change means he isn't getting better, either. It's like he doesn't even care if I'm here."

"He'll get better, Chris," Parker said. "I wish I could come over, but Sam and Tor are nuts getting ready for Meadowlark."

"That's okay," she said. "You should be really proud that your own students are already at training level."

Parker groaned. "Do you remember the first time I competed at Meadowlark?"

Christina exhaled heavily. "You mean the time you and Foxy didn't quite make the drop jump through the old hay barn?" Christina shook her head at the memory. Parker's bay mare had somersaulted onto him, breaking Parker's arm and chipping a bone in Foxy's leg. But they had both recovered, and continued to compete successfully.

"I hope all you guys do well today," Christina said.

"Thanks, Chris," Parker replied. "I'll be by as soon as I can."

Christina walked down to the office to put the phone away. She saw Cindy sitting on a bale of hay just outside the barn door.

"How's your arm?" she asked, poking her head out the door.

Cindy looked up, a hard expression on her face. "It's fine," she said irritably. "You'd think I had major surgery or something, the way everyone keeps trying to baby me. It's driving me nuts. All I want to do is ride, and no one will let me."

Christina shrugged. She was getting used to Cindy's ferocious outbursts. "If you feel like visiting,

119

I'll be at Star's stall," she said, not sure she wanted Cindy's company, but still trying to be polite.

As she headed back through the barn she picked up an armful of bridles that needed cleaning. She checked Star over again, giving him fresh water and offering him some sweet feed. He nibbled a little at the handful of grain, then turned his head away.

Christina sat down in front of his stall, sick with worry. If Star didn't start eating more, his recovery would take that much longer. It would take weeks for him to build up his strength again.

She heard the office phone ring, and Cindy came down the aisle toward her, holding the cordless phone. Her eyes were wide and excited, and she pressed the receiver into Christina's hand.

Christina held the phone to her ear. "Hello?"

"Christina Reese?" a woman asked.

Christina didn't recognize the voice.

"This is Connie Richmond," the woman said. "I'm Ben al-Rihani's trainer. You remember, you beat our colt, Rush Street?"

"Yes, of course I remember," Christina said, sitting up straight. "We met in the restaurant in New York."

"I'm calling to see if you'd be interested in riding Rush Street for us," Connie said. "Mr. al-Rihani and I were so impressed by your skillful riding last weekend, we hoped we could talk you into racing our colt."

Christina felt her jaw go slack. Race Rush Street? She stared at Cindy, her mind reeling. Behind her, the bedding in Star's stall rustled as the colt shifted his weight.

Remembering her priorities, Christina slowly shook her head. "I'm sorry, Ms. Richmond," she said. "I'd love to race your horse for you, but I don't think I'll be coming up to Belmont for a while."

Cindy's eyes widened in disbelief, and her jaw dropped.

Christina ignored her, explaining about Star and telling the trainer that she had to stay home to look after him. She thanked Connie for the offer, then hung up the phone.

"I can't believe you just did that!" Cindy exclaimed, shaking her head in amazement. "First Vince Jones, and now Ben al-Rihani?"

Christina squinted at her. "Don't you get it? I can't leave until I know Star is all right," she said. "He needs me here."

"But you're turning down a chance to ride one of the al-Rihani horses—no one does that!"

Christina stared at Cindy. "I don't care about riding any horses right now," she said. "I can't go back to New York while Star is sick. I'd be worthless on the track. All I'd be thinking about is how he was doing."

"Christina, get real," Cindy said tersely. "He's getting the best medical attention in the world, and he isn't left alone for a second. Riding for the al-Rihanis is the opportunity of a lifetime. First a race at Belmont, and the next thing you know, you'll be in Dubai racing the whole al-Rihani string! I'd give anything to get on the track again, and you're just sitting here, letting these amazing chances pass you by."

Christina bit her lower lip and shook her head. "Star means more to me than anything else," she said. "And maybe you don't see it, but he needs me here. I can't leave him."

Cindy whistled softly. "Then I hope he pulls through for you, Chris," Cindy said. "I really do, because you're turning your back on the biggest break you might ever be offered."

"But I thought you didn't like the al-Rihanis," Christina countered. "Why do you care if I ride for them or not?"

"Ben al-Rihani and I were both barely eighteen when I went back to Dubai to work at his father's stable," Cindy said. "Champion and I had already won the Dubai Cup, and the al-Rihanis' stable manager gave me a job working with some of their Thoroughbreds. Sheik al-Rihani himself told me I had a wonderful way with the horses. But when it came time to select jockeys for the races, Ben convinced his father that it was a bad idea for a young woman to race against the men. I heard them discussing it. I was so angry, I quit right away. That's when I came back to New York to race. And I've regretted it ever since. I should have stuck around and proved to them that I was good enough to compete with the men."

"But he offered *me* a chance to ride for him," Christina said, confused.

Cindy raised her eyebrows. "Ben has obviously changed his attitude about women jockeys, Chris. But now that you've turned him down, I doubt he'll ask you again. He's too proud for that. You just refused an offer from the owner of the best horses in the world."

Christina stared evenly at Cindy. "I've already ridden the best horse in the world," she said, glancing over her shoulder at Star, who stood quietly in his stall. "I've ridden Wonder's Star."

Cindy smiled and relaxed her stance a little. "All right, Chris, I hear you. It's just hard to see you missing such a great chance." She clutched her bad shoulder. "Until you've been told you can't race, it's hard even to see what you're missing. I wish you'd reconsider the al-Rihanis' offer."

"I can't," Christina said. It seemed ironic that she was perfectly healthy and was turning down the chance to race some top Thoroughbreds, while Cindy would do anything to get back on the track but couldn't.

Christina knew in her heart, though, that she

123

couldn't desert Star. She looked steadily at Cindy. "I know you'd do the same thing if you were in my place," she said. "I'm not going anywhere until I know Star is all right."

Cindy walked off, shaking her head, and Christina turned back to the colt.

"I'm here with you, Star," she said, rubbing her hands along his neck. She kept up the massage, determined to do anything that might help the colt. But she was desperately afraid that what little she could do might not be enough.

9

ON MONDAY MORNING CHRISTINA WENT STRAIGHT TO Star's stall. The colt was standing in the far corner, his ears drooping, leaning his weight against the wall of the stall. He looked exhausted.

"He's been like that all night," Jonnie said, rising as Christina opened the stall door. "Just standing there against the wall."

"Thanks for staying with him," Christina said to the sleepy-eyed groom.

"Anytime," Jonnie said with a friendly smile. "Is there anything else I can do for you?"

"No, thanks," she replied. "Get some sleep."

Jonnie walked away, leaving Christina alone with the listless colt. Christina inhaled deeply, trying to steady herself before she approached the dejected-looking horse.

"Star," she said, forcing a cheerful tone to her voice. "Hey, boy, I brought you a nice juicy apple."

But the colt didn't respond, and Christina started to tremble as she ran her hands along his shoulder. "You need to hang in there, boy," she said softly, afraid she was going to dissolve into tears.

"Dr. Stevens will be here soon," Ashleigh said, stopping outside Star's stall. "We're his first stop of the morning."

Christina looked over her shoulder. "Star's getting worse," she said, unable to keep the anguish from her voice.

"He's still on his feet," Ashleigh said. "That's a good sign." She consulted the clipboard she was holding, then looked back up at Christina. "I want you to do your regular works today," she said. "Naomi is leaving for Turfway first thing this morning, so we're short on riders. I'll have Cindy keep an eye on Star."

Christina froze. Not Cindy. She was way too wrapped up in her own problems to pay any attention to Star. Star looked as though he was on his last legs. He needed kindness and encouragement, not harsh words. "Please, Mom, let me stay with him," she begged.

"Cindy will take good care of him," Ashleigh said. "She really does have a way with the horses, Chris."

126

Christina's protest died on her lips as Ashleigh walked away at a brisk pace.

"I have to go, Star," she said, hugging his head to her. "But I'll be back as soon as I'm done."

As she left the stall Cindy came down the aisle, a magazine and a cup of coffee in her hands.

"He's very sensitive," Christina started to say, but the sour look on Cindy's face stopped her.

Maureen was waiting by the track with Leap of Faith, a two-year-old filly who had a lot of promise. Christina adjusted her stirrups and rode Faith onto the track, where Melanie was already riding Pride's Heart clockwise on the outside rail.

Christina jogged the filly around the track as the sun rose on the horizon. On any other morning she would have enjoyed watching the play of colors on the skyline, but today the beautiful gold and rose streaks of sunlight on the dark horizon seemed flat and muddy.

Melanie rode up beside her, checking her chestnut colt until they were keeping pace with Faith. "How is Star doing this morning?" she asked.

Christina shrugged, tightening her left rein as Faith tried to get ahead of Heart. "Cindy's keeping an eye on him," she said flatly.

Melanie frowned. "I tried to ask her about riding at Belmont, and she just about bit my head off."

"I know," Christina said. "I wish Mom didn't insist on having her watch Star. I don't think Cindy really likes horses all that much."

Melanie darted Christina a sympathetic look. "I have to take Heart back," she said, bobbing her head toward the gap in the rail, where Joe was holding Raven. She left Christina to finish Faith's workout.

When Christina returned to the barn, Cindy was still seated outside Star's stall, flipping through the pages of her magazine. She looked bored, and Christina wondered if she'd even looked at Star once the whole time she'd been there.

Christina took a step toward Star's stall, but her mother's voice stopped her. "You need to get your chores done and go to school, Chris," Ashleigh called out from the barn office. "Star will be fine with Cindy."

Christina ached to return to Star's side. Instead she finished her chores automatically and moved through the school day feeling like a zombie.

When she got home, Dr. Stevens's van was pulling out of the driveway. Christina rushed to the barn, and Ashleigh met her in the doorway, looking harried.

"What is it?" Christina demanded, her heart frozen. "What's happened to Star?"

Ashleigh caught her by the arm as Christina started to rush past her. "Star's still hanging on," she said. "Cindy's with him."

"What did Dr. Stevens say?" Christina demanded.

Ashleigh pressed her lips together in a hard line. "Dr. Stevens says they've narrowed the source of the virus down to Fire 'n' Ice and one other horse in Florida."

"And how are they doing?" Christina asked desperately.

Ashleigh sighed. "Fire 'n' Ice isn't doing so well," she said, shaking her head. "And the one down in Florida . . . he didn't make it."

The rush of horror that swept through Christina left her dizzy. "No," she gasped. "There must have been something else wrong with him. Star's going be fine. I know he is."

But the solemn expression on Ashleigh's face frightened her even more. "He's going to pull through this," Christina insisted, pulling away from her mother and hurrying through the barn.

Cindy was seated in front of Star's stall, a pile of tack at her feet and a can of leather cleaner in her hand. She looked up as Christina neared, then turned her attention back to her work.

Christina paused, taking several deep breaths to calm herself. She didn't want to stress Star by letting him see how upset she was.

Cindy put down the bridle she was cleaning and stood up. "If you're going to be here with him for a while, I have some other things to do," she said brusquely.

"Thanks for staying with him," Christina answered as Cindy walked away. She wished with all her heart that she had been there to watch over the colt all day instead of Cindy.

"Hey, boy," she said softly, stepping into Star's stall. Star swung his head toward her and breathed deeply. In the time he'd been home, his coat had started to lose its luster, and his mane looked limp and dull. Star groaned softly, and Christina draped her arm over him protectively. The thought of losing her beloved colt terrified her.

"You can do this, boy," she murmured, blinking back tears. "You can beat this."

Star sighed softly, and Christina kept up her gentle pats and flow of encouraging words for several minutes.

"Let's walk a bit, boy," she said eventually, trying to keep Star's attention. She clipped his halter and lead in place and led him into the aisle. They started out walking slowly but steadily, but partway down the aisle, Star staggered, barely able to keep his feet.

"Are you all right?" Christina asked anxiously, running her hand along his side. "You've been spending too much time standing in your stall, I think." But she knew that wasn't it. He'd been out walking every day. Christina walked forward again, and Star started after her. To her dismay, Star's hind legs wobbled with each step as he struggled to keep from stumbling.

"Oh, no, Star," Christina moaned, stopping him. When she called for her mother, both her parents and Ian came running from the other end of the barn.

"Walk him out again," Ashleigh said tersely, stepping back to watch Star closely.

It cost the colt a huge effort to take a single step. Christina knew how hard he was trying, but his whole body trembled as he struggled to walk in a straight line.

"Get him back into his stall," Mike said. "I'll call for the vet."

Dr. Stevens was at a neighboring farm, and he arrived at Whitebrook in a matter of minutes.

"This is not good," he said, watching Star wobble on his hind legs. "The loss of control means whatever is making him sick is putting pressure on his spinal column." He shook his head grimly, then glanced at Ashleigh and Mike. "We'll do everything we can to keep him comfortable, and give him something to keep the swelling down, but he's going to have to fight this off on his own."

Christina yearned for a miracle, but so far all Dr. Stevens could offer were medications, and they didn't seem to be doing anything to help.

After the vet left, she began giving the colt another massage. Star stood still, his head low, as though he didn't have the strength to hold it up. But he tilted his chin so that he was looking at Christina.

She gazed into his dark, trusting eyes and choked on a sob. "I'm here for you, boy," she murmured, rubbing his weak legs. "I'm right here."

"You're supposed to do your chores," Cindy told her from outside the stall. "I told your parents I'd keep an eye on him for you." Christina glanced up at her, and Cindy flashed a thin smile. "He's a fighter, Chris. If any horse can overcome this, he can."

"Thanks, Cindy," Christina said, giving Star's forehead a gentle rub before she left the stall.

When she was nearly to the office she realized she had forgotten to pick up Star's brushes and disinfect them before returning them to the tack room. But when she reached the isolation area Cindy's chair was empty except for the magazine she had been reading. Christina clenched her jaw, irritated that Cindy would leave Star, even for a minute.

But as she stood in the aisle Christina heard a faint sound. She listened intently, then realized it was a woman's voice, singing. She took a step closer and cocked her head, trying to figure out where the music was coming from. Then she realized it was coming from Star's stall. Had Cindy left the radio on to keep

Star company while she left him alone?

Christina peeked over the edge of the stall. Cindy was standing in the corner of the stall, stroking Star's nose and singing softly to him.

Christina stood there for a minute, then slipped away quietly. Star seemed to be in good hands. She hurried through her chores before returning to the stall.

Cindy was just stepping outside. Her face looked softer and less stressed than it had since she'd come home. She leaned on the door of the stall, watching as Christina offered Star a warm bucket of mash.

"I've spent so much time exercise riding and racing," Cindy said, "I'd forgotten what it's like to just spend time with a horse." She shook her head when Star turned up his nose at the bucket of food. "Don't let him fool you, Chris," Cindy said. "He hasn't given up yet."

"Thanks," Christina said, amazed at the change in Cindy. She put down the bucket and ran her hand along Star's neck. His skin was loose, a clear sign of dehydration. Christina pulled his ear affectionately, but Star didn't react.

The faint spark of hope Cindy's words had kindled was instantly smothered. Star appeared to be getting worse.

10

IT WAS GETTING DARK WHEN CHRISTINA FINALLY LEFT THE barn. Her parents had gone up to the house hours earlier. Star lay quietly, not showing any signs of change.

"I won't leave him for a minute," Joe promised, holding up a magazine and a large mug of muddy-looking coffee. "I'll be right here all night long."

"Thanks, Joe," Christina said, still reluctant to leave Star's side.

When she walked outside, Cindy was sitting on a bale of hay near the barn door, a glum look on her face. "How's Star?" she asked.

Christina sat down beside Cindy and looked up at the pale stars sparkling in the night sky. An almost full moon shed its silvery light over the farm, creating a stark, colorless landscape. "He's still the same," she answered.

"I sure hope he pulls through this, Chris," Cindy said sincerely. "I know how much you love him."

Cindy's words startled Christina. She'd thought Cindy was so wrapped up in her own problems that she was completely oblivious to what was going on around her. It was odd to think that Cindy, who had seemed so gruff and irritable, really did care.

"Thanks, Cindy." For a moment they sat together in companionable silence. Then Christina looked over at Cindy.

"I heard you and Ian talking about your shoulder," Christina said. "I hope you get better quickly so you won't miss too much racing."

Cindy grimaced. "I'm going to be missing a lot of racing," she said. "I have a torn rotator cuff, and I'll probably need surgery to fix it."

Christina felt her jaw drop. "But that will take a long time to recover from."

Cindy nodded, releasing a shaky sigh. "It could take a year," she said, swallowing hard. "Or it could be never."

"I'm so sorry," Christina said.

"It isn't exactly anything new," Cindy said. "I've been fighting it for years. But I've never been a quitter."

Christina smiled. "Just like Star," she said.

Cindy nodded. "Just like Star. Neither of us is going to give up easily."

"So what are you going to do now?" Christina asked.

Cindy shrugged. "I'll play it by ear for a while," she said. "If I can't ride, there's no reason to rush back up to New York." She glanced around her, taking in the soothing sights and sounds of Whitebrook at night. "There are worse places I could be than here." She stood up. "I'm going to bed. I'll see you later, Chris."

"Good night," Christina said, watching Cindy walk toward the McLeans' cottage. Then she headed for her own house. The golden light spilling from the windows looked like bright, warm beacons.

Melanie was waiting for her in the kitchen. "Are you okay?" she asked anxiously. "I didn't want to bother you while you were with Star."

Christina shook her head. "I won't be okay until Star is," she said.

"Everyone else went to bed," Melanie said.

Christina nodded. "Thanks for waiting up for me, Mel."

"I put a plate of food in the refrigerator for you," Melanie said. "Do you want me to heat it up?"

Christina shook her head glumly. "I'm not hungry," she said. "Thanks anyway, Mel."

She wanted to tell her cousin about Cindy, but all of a sudden she felt too tired even to speak. All of her energy had gone into Star. Christina yawned heavily and headed for the stairs.

The next morning Christina awoke with a start, amazed that she had slept so soundly. She dressed quickly and hurried down to the barn. Melanie had Catwink out and was grooming her. Joe and Jonnie were mucking stalls. Christina started toward Star's stall, then stopped when she saw her mother standing in the office. Christina stepped inside.

"I was thinking," she said to Ashleigh. "Since you and Ian and Maureen are so busy getting the yearlings started, why don't you have Cindy manage the morning works? With everything she knows, she might be the perfect new assistant trainer."

Ashleigh stared at her for a moment, then a slow smile spread across her face. She nodded. "What a great idea, Chris. I'll ask her," she said.

Christina left the office and hurried to Star's stall. The colt was standing up now, his nose near the door.

"Hey, spoiled boy," she said affectionately, relieved when he flicked his ears and lifted his nose toward her. "Are you feeling better?" she asked. "I'm going to fix your breakfast." She headed back down the barn to the feed room.

When she stepped back into the aisle a few minutes later, a pan of mash in her hands, Ashleigh and Cindy were standing in the office doorway. Cindy was wearing a Whitebrook cap and held a clipboard. "I'll compare the times as soon as the horses are done working," she told Ashleigh, looking over the roster of horses on the schedule.

"Great," Ashleigh said. "We can go over the numbers later."

Ashleigh went back into the office, and Cindy flashed Christina an excited grin. "Your mom asked if I'd help supervise the morning workouts. She and Naomi are going to start backing a couple of the yearlings, and my dad had to go to Keeneland. At least it's better than sitting around doing nothing."

"That's great," Christina said, pleased at the bright look on Cindy's face. "I'll be out to ride my horses as soon as I finish feeding Star."

"That's fine," Cindy said. "I'll see you on the track." She walked off, a little spring in her step.

Christina returned to Star's stall with a pan of warm mash. He nosed around the feed with some interest while she held the pan, and he actually chewed and swallowed a few bites. He looked ten times as animated as he had the night before, which still wasn't saying much. "That's it," she encouraged. "You just eat it all up, boy."

Ashleigh came down to the stall and watched approvingly as Star chewed on a mouthful of grain. "He sure looks good this morning," she said. "Have you tried walking him yet?"

Christina shook her head. "But he's a lot perkier than he was yesterday," she said. "That last dose of vitamins Dr. Stevens gave him must have helped him fight the virus off."

"Don't get ahead of yourself, Chris," Ashleigh warned. "He's still very weak."

But Christina just beamed back at her mother. "Look at him," she said. "He's eating and he's alert." She nodded confidently. "It's going to take some time, but he's going to be ready for the Fountain of Youth Stakes in February. I know he will."

Ashleigh gazed at the colt for a moment before she spoke. "Maybe you're right," she said, and then headed back down the aisle.

"You're coming out of this, aren't you, boy?" Christina asked, shaking the pan a little. Even though he had shown more interest in his food than he had in several days, she knew he wasn't eating enough. She ran her hand along his side, disturbed to feel the ribs so close to the skin. "You need to start eating a little more," she said, stroking his neck. "It's going to be harder to recover if you lose any more weight."

Star flicked an ear at her and pressed his nose into

139

the grain pan, chewing thoughtfully on another small mouthful.

"That's it!" Christina said. "Just a little more. Come on, boy."

But Star didn't take any more bites, and finally she set the pan aside. "I'd better get out to the track," she said. "I'll check on you one more time before I leave for school."

Star grunted softly, then dropped his head and sighed.

Christina hated to leave him, but Joe and Jonnie were just a few yards away. She went through the routine of exercising her assigned horses, then cleaned their tack. After she was done with her regular chores, she stopped by the office. Cindy was at the desk, going over papers.

"You look like my mom sitting there," Christina teased her.

Cindy glanced up and smiled. "I'm just comparing the morning workouts," she said. "Dad is talking about taking Raven to Keeneland next week." She gazed wistfully at a picture of her and Champion on the office wall, in their moment of glory after the Dubai Cup. "I'd love a chance to race for Whitebrook again."

Christina didn't know what to say. She could tell by the look on Cindy's face that she knew the chances of her racing again so soon were nearly nonexistent.

The phone rang, and Cindy picked it up. "White-brook Farm," she said, then paused. "Christina? May I ask who's calling?" When she heard, Cindy grinned at Christina and covered the mouthpiece. "It's Parker Townsend," she mouthed, her eyes twinkling. "Are you here?"

Christina nodded vigorously, trying to grab the phone from Cindy.

"Just a moment," Cindy said, holding out the receiver.

"Parker!" Christina pressed the phone against her ear.

"How's Star?" Parker asked first.

Christina sighed. "He's eating a little," she said. "He looked terrible last night, but he seems to have more energy today."

"I wondered if you wanted to take a quick drive to Keeneland after school," Parker asked. "My parents bought a new colt at the auction, and they're leaving him there to start him on the track. He sounds pretty cool, and I thought you might want to check him out."

Parker had never shown any interest in his parents' Thoroughbreds. Either this colt was pretty special or Parker was just trying hard to make her feel better. "I don't know," she said slowly. "I don't want to leave Star alone."

Cindy grabbed the phone from her. "She'd love to

go, Parker," she said. "I'll stick right beside Star the whole time she's gone. Don't take no for an answer." She handed the phone back to Christina.

"Sorry about that, Parker," Christina said. "Cindy lost control of herself for a moment."

Parker laughed. "I guess that means you'll go?"

"Sure," Christina said. "Star seems to be doing better, and Mom and Cindy will be here to keep an eye on him." It felt good to say Cindy's name as if she was a friend now.

After school Parker met her in the student parking lot. He opened the pickup's door so that she could climb onto the seat.

"I'm glad you decided to go," Parker said. "I know you hate to leave Star for very long, but you need to get out a little, too." He narrowed his eyes and looked at her closely before he started the truck. "When was the last time you ate? You look like you could use some good food."

"You mean you want a burger, right?" Christina said with a laugh.

"You know me too well," Parker said, pulling onto the road. "They don't feed me right at home. I want a greasy fast-food cheeseburger and a big order of french fries."

142

"Me too," Christina said, surprised to realize she had an appetite. "And a strawberry shake."

They stopped for hamburgers on their way to the track, getting their order at the drive-through window, then parking in the lot to eat.

"The dashboard diner," Parker said, laying out paper napkins for their food. "My favorite fine restaurant."

Christina fed Parker french fries one at a time, until finally he grabbed the fry box from her. "Too slow!" he exclaimed, stuffing a handful into his mouth at once.

"Pig," Christina laughed, digging into her own paper-wrapped burger.

When they reached the track, Parker pulled into the backside lot and they headed for Townsend Acres' stables.

Christina gazed around her, watching the familiar backside activity. Racing was going to start at Keeneland in just a few days, and most of the trainers had horses at the track, preparing them for the upcoming fall meet. It was strange not to be a part of all the action. A spirited chestnut colt danced at the end of a lead line, scooting its hindquarters to the side and shying at nothing. The colt reminded Christina of the way Star used to be when he was impatient to get out on the track. *The way he'll be again,* she amended.

When they stopped at the Townsends' stalls,

Christina glanced around, spotting a gray nose sticking out of one stall. "Is that him?" she asked.

"That's him. He's called Celtic Mist," he said, walking to the stall door.

The dark gray colt threw his nose up, testing the air, then released an ear-shattering whinny.

Christina laughed, pressing her hands to her ears. "Well, he sure is loud," she said.

Celtic Mist arched his sleek dappled neck and shoved his nose in her direction. Christina touched the colt's delicate nose, marveling at the perfect beauty of his head. He was handsome, but he wasn't as magnificent as Star. No horse ever would be.

"Hello, Parker. I see you brought Christina to see our new investment."

When she heard Brad's voice, Christina cringed. Then she turned to face Brad and Lavinia. The Townsends stood in the aisle, looking as though they were ready for a photo session in the winner's circle. Lavinia's clothes were the height of fall fashion, and her hair was styled perfectly, with not a single strand out of place.

Christina hated the way just being near Lavinia made her feel inferior. She darted a glance at Parker, whose face was unreadable. "Hello, Mother," he said with a polite smile, leaning forward to kiss her cheek.

"No, no!" Lavinia said, shooing him back. "You've

been touching the horse. You're filthy."

Christina grimaced. How Lavinia could be so cold to her only child was beyond her understanding.

Parker took a step back, a hurt expression on his face, and Christina ached for him. She glanced at Lavinia, trying not to let her feelings show. "Your new colt is beautiful," Christina said honestly. "I'll bet he can run, too."

"We wouldn't have bought him otherwise," Lavinia said, looking down her nose at Christina. "Not that we needed your opinion of his ability." She glanced at Parker. "Are you going to be home this evening? We're having a small dinner party, and I wasn't sure if we could count on you."

Parker shook his head. "I'll be cleaning stalls over at Whisperwood," he said.

Christina bit down a smile at the look of disgust on Lavinia's face.

Brad pointed at the majestic gray colt and nodded at Christina. "I decided I needed to invest in a new colt so that Townsend Acres can be sure to have something of Derby caliber," he said.

Christina frowned. "We have Star," she said. "He's going to be in the running."

"*We* do not have Star," Lavinia corrected her. "Your parents have half, and we have half. You need to remember you're the colt's jockey, not his owner.

Besides, Brad tells me Star is very sick."

Christina lifted her chin and met Lavinia's cool gaze with one of her own. She was about to respond when Brad spoke up.

"Yes, and speaking of that," Brad said, resting a hand on Lavinia's arm, "I wondered if you were still interested in buying my half of Star, Christina."

As shocked as Christina was at Brad's words, Christina felt a small degree of satisfaction when she saw that Lavinia's eyes widened in surprise, too.

"You'll sell your half of Star to me?" she asked, staring at Brad in confusion.

Brad nodded. "With the full knowledge, of course, that he may never recover from this illness."

"That doesn't matter to me," Christina said. "But I still don't have nearly enough money to pay what he's worth."

Brad pulled a small leather-bound notepad from his jacket pocket. With a thin gold pen he scribbled a few quick lines on a page.

"Upon receipt of this amount," he said, tearing the sheet from the pad and handing it to Christina, "my ownership in Star is all yours."

"Why are you doing this?" Parker demanded, his tone suspicious.

"As I told Christina," Brad said, "it's doubtful Star will recover."

146

Brad seemed to be acting out of pity, although Christina didn't think he had it in him. So Brad didn't think Star would pull through. Well, she didn't care what he thought. His offer was too good to refuse.

"It doesn't matter, Parker," Christina said, staring at the paper. She had far more than the amount Brad had stated as Star's price. She looked at Brad again. "I'll have the money for you tomorrow," she said quietly, tucking the note in her pocket.

"And I'll have the transfer papers done up this afternoon," Brad replied.

"I don't understand why you're doing this," Christina said despite herself. "Star is still holding his own. Dr. Stevens seems to think he'll turn around and make a full recovery in time for the winter races." She knew she was stretching the truth, but Dr. Stevens had never said Star wouldn't race again.

Brad shook his head, giving her a look of pity. "Apparently you haven't heard."

"Heard what?" Christina asked, her heart thudding dully in her chest at the ominous tone in Brad's voice.

Brad shook his head. "Just before we came over here, I got a call from Belmont. The colt that was stabled next to Star died a few hours ago."

11

PARKER CAUGHT CHRISTINA BY THE ARM AS SHE STAGGERED back, reeling from Brad's blunt statement. She stared at Brad, her heart filled with dread.

Brad seemed oblivious to her reaction. "I didn't realize you were unaware that the other colt had died," he said calmly. "In that case, I won't hold you to the purchase of Star." He held out his hand, waiting for her to return the piece of paper.

Christina shook her head stubbornly. "No," she said. "I'm buying him." She turned to Parker. "I'm ready to go home now."

"All right. Come on, Chris," Parker said, wrapping his arm around her. "Let's get out of here."

Without a word to his parents, Parker turned her away.

As they walked off, Lavinia's voice rose as she spoke to her husband, and they could hear her clearly. "What were you thinking?" she snapped at Brad. "You just gave that colt away!"

Brad's voice rang out clearly. "I know," he said. "But the insurance we have on him doesn't even cover this situation. He's worth more to us as a tax write-off."

Christina stiffened, but Parker kept his arm around her, propelling her toward his truck.

"I'm so sorry," he said. "I never would have brought you here if I knew they were coming. Please forgive me, Chris." He opened the passenger door. Christina sat stiffly on the seat, staring out the windshield.

"It wasn't your fault, Parker," Christina said as he climbed behind the wheel. She was still trying to comprehend the meaning of what Brad had said, but her mind could barely grasp the idea that losing Star was becoming a likelihood.

"This doesn't mean Star is going to . . . you know," Parker mumbled.

"At least I'm going to own him now," Christina said, closing her hand around the piece of paper Brad had written up. Her dream had come true, but at what price?

When they reached Whitebrook, Parker stopped his truck near the barn, and Christina jumped out to hurry inside.

Ashleigh was leaning against Star's stall, staring inside. Christina felt a wave of dizziness come over her as she rushed to her mother's side. She took a deep breath before she looked into the stall, terrified of what she might see. But Star looked just the way he had when she'd left in the morning. He was standing as still as a statue, listless but alive.

She heaved a sigh of relief and went into the stall. "You're not going to die, Star," she said firmly, burying her face in his drooping neck.

"Dr. Stevens just left," Ashleigh said, her voice flat.

Christina looked up at her mother, her heart filled with dread. "What did he say about Star?"

"That as long as he's still on his feet, we have hope."

Parker came up and stood next to Ashleigh. The looks on both their faces made Christina turn away. She didn't want the pity she saw in their eyes, or the sadness. "Star is going to be fine," she said stubbornly. "I know he is."

Ashleigh squeezed her hand and left them alone.

Parker stayed there, leaning on the door. "There's one thing Star has that the other horses didn't," he offered.

Christina ran her hand along one of Star's limp ears before she looked up at him. "What's that?" she asked.

Parker nodded at her. "You. Star has you, Chris, and he'll pull through this because of you."

"I hope so," she replied, rubbing her hands along the colt's neck.

"Look, I need to get over to Whisperwood," Parker said. "I promised Sam I'd take care of the barn while she and Tor go check out some new horses. Promise to call me if you need anything?"

Christina nodded solemnly, not trusting herself to speak.

After Parker left, Christina busied herself giving Star a thorough grooming, sickened by the dull, flat texture of his normally glossy coat.

"You're mine now, Star," she said quietly. "Brad can never tell us what to do with you again. And you'll never leave Whitebrook. Or me."

But Star didn't respond to her voice, and Christina's heart sank lower than she had ever thought possible. When she was done grooming Star, she mixed his feed, loading it with supplements and some extra oil.

"We're going to fatten you right up, Star," she promised, walking back to his stall. But when she reached the door, Star had his back to her, his head stuck in the far corner.

"Star," she said anxiously, but he didn't respond. "Star!" she said more loudly. The colt groaned, barely able to move his head enough to see her. He shifted his weight and tried to turn, but he swayed, nearly crashing to the stall floor. The wall was the only thing that kept him from falling.

"No," Christina whispered. "You can't do this." Star groaned again, and his back legs started to buckle. Christina felt the feed pan slip from her hands. The rubber pan thudded to the floor, scattering sticky feed everywhere. Heedless of the mess, Christina wheeled around and ran screaming through the barn. The office was empty, and Christina dashed out the door, racing toward the house. "Mom!" she yelled. "He's worse! Star's getting worse!"

Ashleigh was halfway to the house. She whirled around and ran back to the barn, following Christina to Star's stall.

To Christina's relief, Star was still standing, but he was using the side of the stall to support himself.

"I'll take his temperature while you call Dr. Stevens," Ashleigh said quickly.

It seemed like an eternity, but it was less than half an hour before the vet arrived. Christina stood outside the stall, rubbing Star's shoulder, talking softly to him. "You're a fighter, Star," she said. "You need to fight this. Do it for me, boy. Do it for us." Star looked at her, the keen intelligence still shining in his eyes.

"You know what's going on, don't you, boy?" she

152

asked. "You know you can't just give up."

Star pressed his nose weakly into her hand. Christina bit her lip and rubbed his soft nose lovingly.

Dr. Stevens came swiftly and looked Star over, a frown darkening his kind face. He shook his head worriedly. "I just don't know," he said. "I'll give him another dose of vitamin supplements to help keep his strength up. All we can do is keep him on his feet."

"Isn't there anything else you can try?" Christina asked desperately.

Dr. Stevens shook his head. "I know, it sure is frustrating. But I'm afraid the hard part is up to him."

After the vet left, Christina stayed in Star's stall. Ashleigh stood outside, pacing back and forth nervously. "I want you to sleep in the house tonight, Chris," she said. "One of the grooms will be here all night."

Christina shook her head. "I'm staying right here," she insisted. She was afraid that if she left, it would be the last time she saw her colt alive. "He needs me. I wouldn't sleep anyway, not knowing how he's doing."

Ashleigh considered her words for a minute, then nodded in agreement. "Okay," she said. "You win. Let's get the cot out of the storeroom. You can sleep in front of his stall."

Christina laid a warm sleeping bag on top of the cot, but every time she started to doze off, she would jerk awake, sure she'd heard some awful noise from Star. She kept jumping to her feet to check on the colt, but every time she looked into his stall, Star was standing motionless, a distant look in his eyes.

"You stay with me, Star," she said urgently. "Nothing is going to happen to you while I'm here."

Finally she gave up on the cot, curling up in a corner of Star's stall, the sleeping bag wrapped around her. Star rested his nose on her shoulder, and Christina finally fell asleep with the comforting sound of Star's breathing in her ear.

The next morning the sounds of the routine activity in the barn woke her. Christina wiggled her neck, stiff from sleeping upright. Star was still standing over her. She reached up to stroke his nose. "I love you, you big spoiled boy," she said, giddy with relief that he had made it through the night. She got stiffly to her feet and stretched.

"He looks better," Ashleigh said from outside the stall.

"The vitamin booster Dr. Stevens gave him must have helped," Christina said, rubbing Star's ears gently. The colt pushed his nose at her, nuzzling the front of her sweatshirt. "You're going to be fine now, aren't you, boy?"

She went to school feeling lighthearted. Star was going to pull through, and even better, he was hers now. Her euphoric mood lasted through the day. When she'd told her mother about Brad's offer, Ashleigh raced her to the car and gave her a ride to the bank, where they had a check drawn up for Brad. Star was going to be hers, all hers!

"Can we stop by Townsend Acres?" Christina asked excitedly. "I don't want to give Brad a chance to change his mind."

Ashleigh agreeably drove her to the farm. Brad was out, but Christina left the check with Ralph Dunkirk, who gave her a puzzled look when she told him what it was for.

"You must be out of your mind," the trainer said. "You ought to take the money and buy yourself a colt at the next auction."

"I don't want just any colt," Christina said, walking away before he had a chance to reply.

When they returned home, Christina hurried to Star's stall. The colt nickered softly when she walked into the stall. She wrapped her arms around his neck, burying her face in his warm coat. Star's eyes were brighter than they'd been the day before. He really did look better.

When she called over to Whisperwood, Parker answered the stable phone. "How is he?" he asked.

"He's doing so much better," Christina said, her heart light with hope that the crisis had passed. "I hate to say it, but I think your dad made a big mistake."

Dr. Stevens came by in the afternoon, a cautious smile spreading across his face when he saw Star still standing. "He seems to have rallied a little," he said. "I wasn't so optimistic yesterday, but he looks pretty good today."

He gave Star another dose of vitamins and handed Christina some powdered supplements for the colt's feed. When he left, she headed for the feed room to mix up a pan of grain.

When she returned to the quarantine area, she found Cindy sitting in front of Star's stall, looking through a magazine. "I'm glad to see him doing better," Cindy said warmly.

"Me too," Christina said. She carried the grain into his stall and held the pan for him. The colt still wasn't very interested in his food, but he nibbled a few bites.

"How's your shoulder?" Christina asked Cindy, who had stood to watch Star eat.

Cindy wrinkled her nose. "The doctor got the results of my shoulder scan back. He says I definitely need surgery." She smiled at Christina. "But you know, maybe this isn't such a terrible thing."

Christina gaped at her, shifting the grain pan so that Star could take a bite if he wanted to. "I don't understand," she said. "I thought racing was the most important thing in the world to you."

Cindy nodded. "I thought so, too," she said. "But now that I've been back at Whitebrook for a while, I've realized something."

Christina cocked her head and eyed Cindy curiously. "What?"

"As much as I love racing, what I really love is the horses. I'd sort of forgotten that that's why I got into racing in the first place. For the love of horses. It doesn't matter if I never race again. As long as I can be around horses, I'm going to be okay."

Christina nodded, understanding completely.

Cindy reached into the stall to run her hand along Star's forehead. "Samantha asked me to go look at a new filly she and Tor are thinking about buying. I'll see you later, Chris."

For the rest of the afternoon Christina stayed by Star's side, massaging his weak legs, urging him to eat and drink. As evening set in, Star began to look listless again, as though the day had completely exhausted him.

"I'm staying with him," she told Ashleigh when her mother came looking for her.

Ashleigh nodded. "I doubt I could talk you out of it," she said.

Melanie brought two plates to the barn, and she sat

with Christina, eating spaghetti in front of Star's stall. "Do you want me to stay with you tonight?" Melanie offered.

Christina shook her head. "We'll be fine," she said. "Thanks, Mel."

She got her sleeping bag and curled up in a corner of the stall, with Star close by. As the night deepened, Star grew agitated, breathing loudly. The darkness was just beginning to fade into dawn when Star began nudging her with his nose, grunting in her ear. Christina got up to flip the stall light on, turning just in time to see Star collapse.

She dropped to the stall floor, cradling his head on her lap. "Star," she cried. "Get up! You have to get up!"

Star gave a few weak kicks, but Christina knew he didn't have the strength to pull himself back onto his feet. Blinded by tears, she ran to the office to call the house.

In minutes her parents were at the barn, wide awake in spite of their sleep-tousled hair. "I'll call the vet," Mike said, taking a quick look into the stall.

Ashleigh got on her knees at the colt's side, running her hands along his heaving flank. "He's so weak," Ashleigh murmured. She looked up at Christina, her eyes haunted.

"What's going on?" Ian was at the stall, his shirt half buttoned. "I saw all the lights over here." He stared down at Star, and comprehension dawned on his face. He glanced at Christina, shaking his head slowly.

In a few minutes Mike and Dr. Stevens came down the aisle. In spite of the hour, the vet looked alert, his clothes neat and his hair combed. He knelt at Star's side, feeling his limbs and listening to his heart. When he prodded Star's hind leg, the colt kicked weakly.

"That's a good sign," he said, looking up at Christina. "As long as he has feeling in his legs, he isn't completely paralyzed."

Since there was little else he could do for Star, Dr. Stevens left after telling them to call him if there were any more changes.

Christina sat down in the stall beside her mother, who wrapped her arm around her daughter's shoulders. "I'm so sorry, honey," Ashleigh said softly.

"He isn't dead yet," Christina said harshly. "Don't give up on him, Mom."

A tiny smile flickered at the corners of Ashleigh's mouth. "Okay," she said. "We won't. I'll go mix a mash for him if you want to take over here."

Christina pulled Star's head onto her lap and gazed into his eyes. He gazed back at her helplessly, and Christina wanted to break down and cry. But she couldn't let herself. Crying would mean that it was over, and she wasn't going to accept that.

"Is there anything I can do?" Cindy said, leaning over the stall door.

Christina looked up, shaking her head. "I wish there were," she said.

"I'll be in the office working on some schedules if you need anything at all," Cindy offered kindly.

"Thanks, Cindy." After she left, Christina looked back down at Star. The colt lay motionless. "I'm with you, boy," she said softly. Star shifted his head to look up at her, and Christina pressed her lips together and squeezed her eyes shut to hold back the tears that threatened to spill over.

She held her hand against his muzzle, and Star sighed into her palm and kept his gaze on her face. Christina stayed with him that way throughout the morning, hoping for a miracle.

12

THE DAY PASSED WITHOUT CHRISTINA LEAVING STAR'S stall. She heard the routine sounds of the farm in the distance: the rumbling of the tractor they used to drag the track, haul hay to the barns, and carry the used bedding to the composting pit; the clattering of hooves on the barn floor; the whinnying of the horses as they were led from their stalls for the day; the shriller call of the weanlings demanding their breakfast; the familiar voices of the farm workers.

Christina stroked Star's long neck and looked down at him. Star's eyes were open, and he met her gaze. "Poor, sick Star," she said. "I don't want you to suffer, but I couldn't stand it here if you were gone. I don't know what I'd do. Please, can't you get up? Show me that you're not paralyzed."

161

Star lifted his head a few inches, but he didn't have the strength to hold it up. He let it drop heavily back into her lap, and Christina continued to pet him. "You tried, didn't you, boy?" she said, feeling her hope slipping away.

Ashleigh stopped at the stall several times throughout the day. Dr. Stevens came by twice. After he looked at Star the second time, he shook his head sadly and gestured for Ashleigh to step outside with him. Christina couldn't hear what they were saying, but she was afraid she already knew.

The afternoon chores had already been done when Ashleigh stopped by the stall again. "Chris, you need to get some sleep," she said, frowning down at her.

Christina shook her head. Her eyes felt heavy and grainy, her back ached, and a thundering headache pounded at her temples, but she couldn't desert Star. "I can't leave him," she said. "If I go, he'll give up. I know it."

Ashleigh came into the stall and hunkered down beside her. "I'll stay with him while you get some sleep," she said. "You're not going to do Star any good if you collapse from exhaustion."

Christina looked at her mother. She knew she needed to get a couple of hours of sleep. "You won't leave him alone?"

Ashleigh shook her head. "I promise, Chris. I'll stay right by his side until you come back."

Christina slowly unfolded herself, letting Ashleigh take her place at Star's side. The colt settled his head onto Ashleigh's lap like a docile old dog.

Christina stepped out of the stall, then looked back. Star was looking up at Ashleigh, who was crooning softly to him, stroking his shoulder with a gentle hand.

Satisfied that her mother would keep her promise, Christina stumbled up to the house. She staggered upstairs and dropped onto her bed without even taking off her shoes.

"Christina, wake up!"

At Melanie's cry, Christina pushed herself up from the bed, immediately awake. Her heart thudded uncomfortably in her chest as she stared at Melanie, who stood over the bed. The room was dark, and she felt groggy and disoriented.

"What is it?" she gasped, staring wide-eyed at her cousin. "Is it Star? What's happened?"

"You need to get down to the barn," Melanie said urgently, tugging at her arm. "Now."

Christina couldn't inhale. *It can't be.* "He . . . he isn't . . ."

"No," Melanie said. "But your mom wants you to get out there right away."

Christina could tell by her cousin's expression that Star was worse.

Without another word she jumped to her feet and raced down the stairs, Melanie right on her heels.

She was gasping for air by the time she reached the barn, but she ran down the aisle, her soles slapping on the hard floor. When she reached the isolation stall, Ian was standing near the door, looking grim. When he caught Christina's eye, he dropped his gaze, shaking his head ever so slightly.

A sob caught in Christina's throat. She closed her eyes, bracing herself for what she would see when she looked into Star's stall, then gripped the edge of the wall and peered over the door.

Star was still down, his head on Ashleigh's lap. His eyes were closed, and in the shadowy half-light of the stall Christina couldn't tell if he was breathing.

A horrible tearing sensation ripped through her heart, and she felt the tears building behind her eyes. "Mom?" The word came out sounding choked.

Ashleigh looked up. Her face was drawn and pale, her hair loose and tangled with a few bits of straw clinging to it. "I'm sorry, Chris," she said softly. "It looks like he's given up."

"No." The word came out as a low moan. Christina

slipped into the stall, dropping to her knees beside the stricken colt. Ashleigh moved out of the way, letting Christina take the weight of Star's head in her lap. Ashleigh rose slowly, resting her hand on Christina's shoulder.

"Dr. Stevens is on his way," she said, then left the stall.

Christina cradled Star's limp head, stroking his forelock with her fingers. "How can you give up, Star?" she murmured, swallowing around a hard lump in her throat. "We were going to do so many things. I don't even care if you never run again, boy. I don't want to lose you. Please, Star, for me?"

The colt let out a labored groan, seeming to sink deeper into the bedding and away from Christina.

"Oh, no," she cried softly. "No, Star. I can't let you go."

At a sound above her, Christina raised her head. Melanie was looking over the stall door, her eyes sad and shadowed. Ian hadn't moved. He gazed down at Star, looking dejected.

"I wish it didn't have to end like this," he said. "After all you went through to get him this far, it doesn't seem right, Chris."

Ashleigh stood beside Ian, and Mike appeared next to her.

The sound of more footsteps on the aisle had

Christina leaning protectively over Star. She wasn't going to let the vet decide when the colt's life would end. Star wasn't going to go like that.

But no one came into the stall, and she looked up. Kevin and Beth had joined the group outside the stall. Kevin offered Christina a thin smile. "I'm so sorry, Chris," he said. "I wish there were something I could do."

"Thanks, Kev," Christina said.

Cindy rested her chin on the stall door. She caught Christina's eye. Without a word, Christina knew that Cindy understood how she felt.

Christina closed her eyes, trying to transmit her own strength to Star. She felt foolish for even imagining it might work, but she couldn't give up hope. Star groaned weakly, and Christina felt him slip even further away.

She gritted her teeth, trying to resign herself to the terrible fact that she was losing him. She looked up at the people gathered outside Star's stall. All of them she had known all her life. These people, who cared as much about horses as she did, were her family. They had seen Star grow from a sickly foal to a winning racehorse. And now they were here to see him go, offering their support and comfort. She felt her heart swell with gratitude, but more than anything else, she didn't want Star to die.

Star's breathing grew more labored, and Christina sobbed openly. She dropped her head, unable to stop the tears that flowed freely.

They streamed down her cheeks, soaking her face. She screwed her eyes shut, trying to stanch the flow, but the tears broke through, streaming down her cheeks.

Star flinched, and her eyes flew open. This was it. Star was going to try to fight it, then he would be gone. She knew it.

A falling tear hit Star's ear, and the colt flicked his ear irritably.

"Star," Christina said desperately. "Star, listen to me. I love you so much, and I know you love me. I *know* you do."

At her soft words, Star flicked his ear again.

"Try, Star," she whispered. "Just try to hang on. You can get through this. Think of it as a race, boy," she said. "You can do it. Come on, Star, dig in a little deeper. You can do it on the track, and you can do it now."

Star swiveled his ear again, picking up the tone of Christina's voice. She began talking to him the way she did when they were racing, urging him to find that extra gear that took him past the rest of the field and over the finish line first.

"That's it, Christina," Mike said excitedly. "Keep talking to him."

"Come on, Star," she said urgently. "Let's go, boy."

Star opened his eyes and stared up at Christina. "Star," she murmured, "can't you hang on? Do it for us, boy."

With tremendous effort Star nudged his nose toward her.

From above, Christina heard a collective gasp from her family and friends.

"Look at him," Ashleigh said, a hint of excitement in her voice. "He's trying, Chris."

"Hello," a new voice said. Christina looked up to see the familiar face of Dr. Stevens.

At that moment Star struggled to raise his head, nuzzling Christina's arm weakly.

"Star," she exclaimed. "Star, you moved!"

"Let me see that," Dr. Stevens said, wedging himself between Melanie and Cindy. He leaned forward, staring intently at the colt.

"Do it again, boy," Christina said, her voice trembling. She rubbed the colt's shoulder encouragingly. "Show us what you've got."

As if he understood, Star bunched his muscles and gave a tiny kick with his hind leg.

"Did you see that?" Christina cried. "He isn't paralyzed!"

"No," Dr. Stevens said. "He isn't paralyzed, and if we can get him up and moving, there's a possibility he'll make it." He paused and looked at Ashleigh. "But I have to tell you, he may never race again."

Christina didn't care. She gazed up at her mother. "We have to try, Mom."

Ashleigh was smiling. "Yes, we do," she said. "He deserves every chance we can give him."

Christina looked down at Star. His eyes were open, his muzzle still touching her arm. "You're going to make it, aren't you, boy?"

The cheer that rose from the people gathered around the stall sounded better to Christina than any roaring crowd after a winning race. She beamed up at them, her heart bursting with joy. "He's going to make it," she repeated happily.

"We're still looking at maybe," Dr. Stevens said cautiously. "I'd say right now that Star's future is still questionable."

Christina beamed down at Star, who nickered weakly. "We're going to win this, Star. We're going to do it together."

In Star's eyes, Christina saw the deep trust the colt had for her. She didn't care if Star never raced again. Now that he belonged to her, they could have a long and happy life together as long as he lived. And in her heart, he would always be a champion.

MARY NEWHALL ANDERSON spent her childhood exploring back roads and trails on horseback with her best friend. She now lives with her husband, horse-crazy daughter Danielle, and five horses on Washington State's Olympic Peninsula. Mary has published novels and short stories for both adults and young adults.